THE WOODE

Dr Sue Asbee is Staff Tutor in Arts and Lecturer in Literature at the Open University. Her published work on the author, *Margiad Evans' The Wooden Doctor: Illness and Sexuality*, appeared in *Welsh Writing in English* (2004). She has also published work on several other women writers including Virginia Woolf and Kate Chopin.

THE
WOODEN DOCTOR

by

MARGIAD EVANS

With an introduction by
SUE ASBEE

HONNO CLASSICS

Published by Honno
'Ailsa Craig', Heol y Cawl, Dinas Powys
South Glamorgan, Wales, CF6 4AH

First published in England by Basil Blackwell in 1933
This edition © Honno Ltd 2005

British Library Cataloguing in Publication Data

A catalogue record for this book is available
from the British Library

ISBN 1 870206 68 1

Published with the financial support of the Welsh Books Council

Cover image by Margiad Evans,
with kind permission of Cassandra Davies

Cover design: Chris Lee Design

Typeset and printed in Wales by
Dinefwr Press, Llandybïe.

Introduction

SUE ASBEE

'if my pen has ever done anything for Wales it
is honoured.'[1]

(Margiad Evans)

The Wooden Doctor was published in March 1933 to
enthusiastic reviews. *The Daily Herald* thought it was 'an
astonishing story'; James Agate in *The Daily Express* said
'Heavens! What characters and what a plot! . . . This young
woman can write', while Compton MacKenzie's *Daily Mail*
review simply urged people to 'read "The Wooden Doctor".
It is really good'. None of the reviewers dwelt on the vivid
and compelling descriptions of pain that Arabella, the central
character, endures, nor the dark hints that these are related
to her sexuality and her love for her doctor, but it is the
power of such descriptions and the psychology behind them
that make the novel so fascinating. In spite of the reviews,
sales never quite lived up to the promise of that initial
reception. *The Wooden Doctor* was neglected, effectively
becoming a lost classic, perhaps partly because of the
'uncompromising harshness' noted by the *Times Literary
Supplement* reviewer, and an unwillingness to delve too far
into or be seduced by Arabella's tormented mind.

The Wooden Doctor is an extraordinary and unusual novel
about dysfunctional family life, obsessive unrequited love,

1. Quoted in Moira Dearnley, *Margiad Evans* (1982), University of Wales
    Press, 70.

and physical pain – all of which hold interest for contemporary readers and critics. The Prelude tells of a childhood fever that triggers Arabella's obsession with Dr Flaherty, a man thirty years her senior. In Part One she is in France, a pupil-teacher studying the language; Part Two sees her return and the onset of her illness; in Part Three she goes to north Wales to research background for her novel. Here a love affair with a young man results in marriage plans, which are summarily abandoned the moment she sees her beloved Doctor once again. That brief description is probably sufficient to show that the story is episodic rather than tightly plotted. It remains unresolved at the end, perhaps another reason why it was not especially popular with the reading public when it first came out. Modernist writers at the time were finding other ways of organising their narratives, de-emphasising plot and embracing open-endedness, but the structure of *The Wooden Doctor* was determined less by the desire to experiment than by Margiad Evans's own life, for it is a fictional autobiography.

Arabella's abdominal pains dominate the narrative; at first Flaherty confidently assures her that she is suffering from cystitis, but the pains endure and the diagnosis remains inconclusive. There is a strong suggestion that their origin is not physical at all, but nervous or hysterical. Writing at the end of the twentieth century Elaine Showalter remarks that 'as medical institutions expel hysteria, literary critics take it up'. The 'hysterical narrative', she says, has become 'one of the most popular formulations of literary criticism. It has grown at the busy crossroads where psychoanalytical theory, narratology, feminist criticism, and the history of medicine intersect'.[2] Any of these approaches provides useful insights into *The Wooden Doctor*, and indeed it is not easy to

---

2. Elaine Showalter, *Hystories* (1997), New York: Columbia University Press, 81.

separate them out. Hysteria, Showalter says, 'cuts across historical periods and national boundaries, poses fundamental questions about gender and culture, and offers insight into language, narrative, and representation'; it is 'a form of expression, a body language for people who might otherwise not be able to speak or even to admit what they feel'.[3] Hysteria is a complex cultural discourse open to multiple interpretations, and it is particularly relevant to Arabella's narrative, which offers few clear explanations.

The childhood fever and a later more mysterious episode requiring the doctor's attention occur before Arabella leaves for France, establishing a pattern of illness. At first sight Arabella seems eloquent on the subject of her feelings – she expresses vividly the physical pain she endures, her love for the doctor, contempt for her father and mother – nevertheless, there are many gaps and silences in her story. Medical science can find no explanation for her condition, and at various times her mother and even her beloved Doctor come to the conclusion that it was her 'nerves that were wrong' (71). Arabella herself comes to believe that she was 'sick in body and mind' (72). If the cause is indeed psychological, what exactly is responsible for generating this cripplingly painful hysteria? If we define hysterical illness as a consequence of the body articulating symptoms of psychic anguish that cannot be expressed in words, Arabella's narrative offers no clear answers. A childhood nightmare she shares with her sister (9) may hint at sexual abuse, perhaps from her alcoholic father; on the other hand relationships with both her parents are sufficiently unhappy to trigger the illness which renders her helpless and demands the kind of attention she has lacked as a child and adolescent. Of her relationship with her mother, for example, Arabella says their 'old devotion' to each other lies 'dead between

---

3. Showalter, op. cit., 7.

us, killed by cruel words, senseless misunderstandings, wild and wicked recriminations' (91-92), while 'our home among the quiet fields became a cage of savagery' (12).

If her formative years lack nurture, the doctor's kindness goes some way to supplying this need. But there is also a sense in which his care provides not so much a solution as part of the continuing problem. Crucially, by the beginning of the twentieth century, 'some physicians had learned that hysteria could be *iatrogenic* – created by the interaction between doctor and patient'.[4] Rhodri Haywood suggests a physical rather than a psychological explanation for this: 'in gynaecological and urological textbooks of the 1930s, cystitis is often held up as an iatrogenic illness, induced through botched surgical interventions and examinations or through the use of unsterilised instruments'.[5] It is possible that both contribute to Arabella's suffering. Her childhood experience of the new doctor's ability to prevent nightmare ('His touch had cheated the terror' p. 9) is perhaps sufficient to begin the cycle of reliance which continues throughout the course of the novel: when she is ill, he comes.

When Arabella confesses her love and receives kind but professional rejection from her doctor, her feelings intensify and significantly she uses images of the body and sickness in an attempt to describe her experience of love: 'it is possible to be happy before loving, perhaps after, but never while that diabolical poison coursed through the veins' (127). Love and medical attention are associated in her mind from an early age with disastrous results for conventional relationships.

The dramatic frontispiece of the novel (which Evans drew, initialling it 'PW' for her given name, Peggy Whistler) focuses

---

4. Showalter, op. cit., 18.
5. Rhodri Hayward, 'Between Flesh and Friendship: Margiad Evans, F. L. Golla and the Struggle for Self', forthcoming.

attention on illness. Executed in blocks of black and white, the illustration depicts a woman in bed. Her face is half in shadow, the side we see depicts strong features and a sensual mouth. The eye is closed but sleep does not seem tranquil. The body is arranged diagonally across the picture space, head and flowing hair occupying the top right hand corner, framed by the suggestion of a pillow and balanced in the right foreground by a nightstand with jug and ewer. The eye is drawn along diagonal lines of composition, interrupted and disturbed by jagged black folds of bedclothes across the woman's abdomen in the centre of the picture, indicating shattering pains and perhaps even the suggestion of a fox's jaws. Representing Arabella in this way foregrounds her suffering in the narrative, and adds resonance to the question: does her illness have a physical or a psychosomatic cause? In hospital she is variously assured by her consultant that her pain must be stopped, and that there is nothing wrong. Another patient describes the agony of her kidney stones – Arabella claims the symptoms as her own.

Elaine Scarry insists on the difficulty of describing pain, claiming that it 'does not simply resist language but actively destroys it, bringing about an immediate reversion to a state anterior to language, to the sounds and cries a human being makes before language is learned'.[6] Scarry also quotes from Woolf's essay 'On Being Ill': 'The merest schoolgirl when she falls in love has Shakespeare or Keats to speak her mind for her, but let a sufferer try to describe a pain in his head to a doctor and language at once runs dry'.[7] Evans's descriptive power refutes this:

---

6. Elaine Scarry, *The Body in Pain: the making and unmaking of the world* (1987), New York: Oxford University Press, 4.
7. Scarry, op. cit., 4.

Suddenly out of the darkness the fox sprang with flaming feet and famished jaws, rending, biting, tearing. I wished that I could faint and be delivered from this agony, but my strength increased the torture (72).

The repeated imagery of the 'fox in a bag scratching and rending to get out' and the claws that penetrate Arabella's sleep (71) gives the narrative coherence of a kind in the absence of a strong plot, and focus interest on psychology rather than action.

The Preface finishes with a chilling description of family life: 'we sharpened our claws in one another's flesh' (xviii). Through the imagery of claws then, her undiagnosed illness is linked to her family situation. Gaps and silences in Arabella's narrative may be interpreted in various ways, suggesting that an abusive relationship with her father, her mother, or possibly even her own guilt about sexual feelings is responsible. Whatever conclusions we reach, it is clear that Arabella's body articulates complex emotional states which cannot otherwise be expressed.[8]

An Enclosed World

Use of first-person narrative generates a sense of claustrophobia in the novel. Readers share the mind of a young woman in the grip of an intense infatuation, circumscribing the world of the novel with no possibility of escape. The immediacy with which the story is told allows no detachment from events described: we experience the torment of

---

8. For further discussion, see Sue Asbee, 'Margiad Evans's *The Wooden Doctor*: Illness and Sexuality', in *Welsh Writing in English*, vol. 9, 2004, pp. 33-49.

dysfunctional family life at first hand. The repressive milieu of Cours Saint-Louis, the school in France, contributes another closed world – as the Bassencourt school does in Charlotte Bronte's *Villette*, written eighty years earlier. The walled garden of Evans's French school, the directrice's jealousies, the young Englishman, and Arabella's distrust of Roman Catholicism also recall *Villette*. *The Wooden Doctor* is set in the twentieth century, but for readers familiar with Bronte's novel *Villette* co-exists and makes its own contribution to the sense of secrets and repression, while Jane Eyre's experiences at Lowood School might be recalled in Arabella's accounts of intense cold and insufficient food.

Evans's technique of repetition also works to convey claustrophobia. Descriptive words – 'cold', 'cruel', 'biting', 'bitter' – are repeated relentlessly, suggesting a mind constantly circling but never making progress. It is a technique she identified in the work of Byron and of Emily Bronte, arguing that they are 'twin poets' in an essay she published in 1948.[9] Quoting from Bronte's poem 'Light up thy Halls' and Byron's 'Incantation', she points out a similarity in the two writers' diction 'even to the constant use and close-set reiteration of certain terse and ordinary words – words which they invest with a vehement and vindictive purpose almost unique in letters'.[10] Evans uses the technique herself: 'Oh it was cold in the house, and in the garden, bitterly, cruelly, cold and lonely' (53); her mother's letter is 'bitter and biting'; Flaherty would not have 'so cruelly condemned' (54); while the girls 'cried bitterly when they returned to school' (55). The intention may not always be vehement and vindictive, but the repetitions certainly help to maintain the emotional tenor of the narrative.

Arabella is a young woman who takes all her clothes off

9. *Life and Letters Today*, vol. 57, 198.
10. ibid., 200.

in the garden (70) and is unembarrassed by the presence of nurses when she is having a bath, indeed, she is happy for them to scrub her back. Mid-nineteenth-century sensibilities may have little in common with such a lack of inhibition, but even without Evans's fascination with Emily Bronte, Arabella can be regarded within a similar literary tradition. Of the three Bronte heroines – Jane Eyre, Catherine Earnshaw, and Lucy Snowe – who could each exclaim, with Arabella, 'I *had* suffered' (70) *Villette*'s Lucy Snowe is perhaps the closest. In *Wuthering Heights* Catherine Earnshaw's voice, even in delusion, is mediated by Ellen Dean's and Lockwood's, narrators who always provide alternative realities, while Lucy Snowe, like Arabella, tells her own story and keeps secrets from her readers. At times one might be forgiven for believing *The Wooden Doctor* to be set in the late nineteenth century, not simply because of the rural setting but because of its Brontesque tone. But Arabella's unconventionality, her lack of modesty – indeed, her exhibitionist tendencies – ultimately place the narrative firmly in the twentieth.

Constant attention to light and shade also plays its part in evoking the enclosed world of *The Wooden Doctor*. A film version of the novel would need little work on this count for Margiad Evans is her own lighting director. Almost every scene is set with candle, lamp, lantern, firelight – or, in the case of Clystow Royal Infirmary, a rare reference to electric light 'reflected in the glaze' of 'the naked wall' (99). That last example comes as a startling exception, reminding us that we are not in a world before electricity. Returning home from her second hospital visit Arabella finds the house in darkness: Esther comes to let her in, 'a lighted candle smoking and dripping grease on her hand' (101). She has been reading ghost stories, 'a fiery flush dyed her cheeks crimson; her features were heavy from the heat'.

Upstairs lying on a sofa her mother is 'glowering in the dark' (101): in this case bad temper metaphorically lends dull red illumination to a darkened room. This perhaps offers a key to the reiteration of candle, lantern, and lamp, for none offer the stark exposure of electric light; each illuminates only selected pools within the darkness – rather like Arabella's single- point-of-view narrative itself. Only in hospital is she subjected to the pitiless glare of electricity, and significantly that sheds no light on her condition.

Music is important too. In hospital the use of bedside earphones lifts Arabella out of her misery:

> I had forgotten the fox, and knives, and moans and surgeons, anaesthetics, morphia, terror and panoply of death. Harps, violins and horns wove a dance. The thick balcony pillar stood out against the deep, living midnight sky like the fragment of a temple. Fancy flew (88).

Her fancy is theatrical – and again lighting is an important part of the theatricality – but this is all part of the affective power music has on her. Significantly the earphones ensure that the experience is not a shared one. In a later episode Schubert's 'Unfinished Symphony' is broadcast on the wireless against a background of inattentive chatter, effectively isolating Arabella in her response to the music as her experience of pain isolates her from those around her: 'Blissfully and heedlessly they chattered through the giant-striding chords, the unearthed melodies, those faint, receding footsteps dropping into distance like averted doom' (129). Meanwhile, rhythm and movement are equally important in the following passage, where Arabella's interest in and attraction to other women is apparent; Mrs de Kuyper dances spontaneously:

> She rose, lifted her skirt above her knees, displaying
> her beautiful straight legs and arched insteps, and
> began to dance. Her feet tapped like castanets, the
> black folds of velvet whirled and swathed her hips.
> . . . She hardly moved a foot, but her whole body
> was in motion (105).

As a child Arabella remarks on the exotic tenant whose
'long silk-covered legs' contrasted 'strangely with our brown
shins and our aunt's stumps' (6), while in hospital (among
countless other instances) she notices a female student who
'swung her hips as she moved like a person dancing a slow,
sensual tango' (95). The narrative which focuses so closely
on her own body also shows an interest in, and fascination
with, other female bodies. Paradoxically this fascination
does not extend to masculine characteristics, for – surprisingly
– there are no comparable descriptions of Flaherty's physical
appearance.

Biography

Distinguishing between biography and fiction presents a
problem for anyone studying the life and work of Margiad
Evans, or Peggy Eileen Arabella Whistler, as she was
named when she was born on 17 March 1909. In real life, as
a young girl, Peggy Whistler fell in love with Dr John
Leeper Dunlop, only really recovering from what amounted
to an obsession after the publication of *The Wooden Doctor*.
Identification between author and characters is more complicated than that simple description might suggest, for the
novel and biography are supplemented by journals, and in
those she refers to herself as Peggy, Margiad, and even
Arabella. In an early draft of *The Wooden Doctor* there are

times when the author forgets she is writing fiction and refers to her character Arabella by her own name of Peggy – 'Arabella' significantly chosen from her own forenames in the first place. Notions of identity, then, are complex in Evans's work, shifting between the usual boundaries critical readers are taught to observe between life and fiction.

Those complexities multiply when the idea of nation is added to the identity equation, for the English Peggy Whistler adopted a Welsh name for her writing, and the Herefordshire Border country as her spiritual home, while at the same time insisting that she had only 'one drop of Welsh blood'.[11] Reviewers of her fiction quickly labelled her as a Welsh writer, or Anglo-Welsh, taking their cue from her name, and the setting of her first novel, *Country Dance* (1932).

She was born in Uxbridge, Middlesex, first visiting Herefordshire with her father when she was nine years old, to stay at her aunt's farm, Benhall, near Ross-on-Wye. The countryside had a profound and lasting effect on her. Walking alongside the river Wye Peggy was moved to an intensity of feeling for the place that far exceeded her ability to articulate it. Some 'powerful emotion began to rise' in her when it was time to leave, 'some desperate adoration'; through a passion of tears she begged her father 'Oh don't, don't take me away from this place'.[12] Two years later circumstances dictated that, together with her younger sister, she return for an extended stay, until eventually the Whistler family was reunited when the parents bought Lavender Cottage at Bridstow, not far from the farm near Ross-on-Wye.

---

11. Ceridwen Lloyd-Morgan, *Margiad Evans* (1998) Bridgend: Seren, 32.
12. 'The Immortal Hospital', National Library of Wales (hereafter NLW), ms 23369C.

Peggy went to the High School in Ross, passed her Oxford Junior exam in 1923 and her school certificate in 1925, at which point she left for France, to teach and to learn the language. She lived and worked at Cours Saint-Denis, a school in Loches, a small town near Tours. The experience was not a happy one, although eventually it provided material for Part One of *The Wooden Doctor*. Back at Lavender Cottage, inspired by discovering Aubrey Beardsley's work, Peggy studied at the Hereford School of Art. Her first published work was, in fact, illustrations for a book of fables, *Tales From the Panchatantra* (1930), and at that time she thought of herself as an artist rather than a writer. She returned to France for some months in 1926, this time staying in a fishing village in Brittany, Bas Poldu, where a community of artists lived and worked. These experiences also appeared in an early draft of *The Wooden Doctor*, but do not survive in the published version. As a young woman, Peggy had several short-term periods of employment as governess or housekeeper that took her away from Bridstow, but she always returned to Lavender Cottage, her home until 1936 when her father's death meant the place could no longer be maintained.

Family life was far from tranquil. Godfrey (her father) drank, and other members of the family in the house were highly strung. The intensity of a highly charged emotional family life is common to all of Margiad Evans's novels. Love is bound up with jealousy and leads to murder in both *A Country Dance* (1932) and *Turf or Stone* (1934). Married couples practise untold cruelty upon one another, while rivalries and bitterness are rife in all kinds of relationships. *Creed* (1936), her last novel, is similarly violent.

The Wooden Doctor begins with a brief fictionalised account of the sisters' time at Benhall, and a comparison with the later (unpublished and much more extensive)

'Immortal Hospital' memoir suggests that the freedom and unconventionality of their young lives for that period was pretty much representative of the reality:

> My aunt sent us to school in Salus. We were always late because we dawdled on the way eating the biscuits she had given us for lunch, playing with the dogs in the road, or searching the hedges and banks for birds' nests. Our egg collection was very large and carefully classified. We never took more than one egg from a nest (5-6).

Some aspects of her account of rural life recall Stella Gibbons's *Cold Comfort Farm* (1932). Cousin Robbie, for example, slept in the oldest wing of the house, his room 'was like a barn':

> It smelt of leather, dung and feathers. . . . Robbie always went to bed in his boots unless it was Saturday night, and his boots were mighty dirty. Into bed with him he took the alarm clock, about half a bushel or so of chaff: and, unforgettably, a large clasp knife to cut bread and cheese. Fearing he might cut or stab himself in his sleep this was always stuck deep into the mattress. The clock, the knife and occasionally the boots we found and sorted each morning, shaking the bedclothes free of chaff out of the ancient barred windows.[13]

Another cousin, Roger, slept with a loaded gun. Life at Benhall may have been unconventional, if not at times downright eccentric, but it provided much-needed security for the sisters.

---

13. 'The Immortal Hospital', NLW, ms 23369C (p. 13).

Peggy's love for the middle-aged Dr Dunlop, paralleled by the fictional Arabella's love for Flaherty in *The Wooden Doctor*, finally lost its power in her early twenties. Late in life Dr Dunlop married for the first time, and eventually Peggy recovered. In 1940 she married Michael Williams, a man she had met while running a guest house some years before. Married life began in Brickhampton, near Cheltenham, but the couple moved to Llangarron, near Ross, in 1941 where Michael did farm work until he joined the navy the following year.

During their separation Evans wrote regular, long, detailed letters to her husband about her daily life. Her minute observation, attention to domestic detail and to the natural world was already apparent in *The Wooden Doctor*:

> My mother was weeding in the garden, throwing the rubbish that she pulled out of the ground into a white enamel bucket with a hole in the side and a rusty handle that she had used for this purpose as long as I could remember. The red chestnut would soon flower. The deep crimson tulips were going over (121).

Such matter came to form the substance of her letters, with detailed descriptions of the changing seasons. The journals which she had long kept were also a repository for reflections on her intense relationship with nature, and she used them as raw material when, unable to finish a fifth novel for Basil Blackwell, she wrote instead the contemplative account of her inner life, *Autobiography* (1943).

In 1950, pregnant with her daughter Cassandra, she was diagnosed as epileptic. Her habit of journal writing provided her with a reliable record of the deterioration of her health: *A Ray of Darkness* (1952) is the story of her epilepsy, recounted 'as an adventure of body and mind . . . most of it exactly as it was written down at the time, for' she adds, 'I have my diaries'.[14] A book she had longed planned on Emily Bronte was finally abandoned owing to her ill health.

When the Williams family moved to Hartfield in Sussex for Michael's work as a teacher, Evans felt homesick and exiled from the countryside that she loved. She endured several periods in hospital until finally a brain tumour was diagnosed in 1956. The unpublished manuscript 'The Nightingale Silenced' records in painful analytical detail her fear that she was going out of her mind. A sympathetic doctor assured her that she was 'not the type' to suffer mental breakdown, a remark which prompted this reflection on her writing:

> It is true that somewhere centrally a calm and solemn detachment persists and has always persisted amid my extravagance, childish frivolity and general muddle-headedness. . . . From this central theme of the spirit has sprung all my work including the tragic and the comic. A person who chatters easily, lightly, to others, I do not speak to myself but left alone, begin to listen to this human tune. . . . It has a great many limitations and has narrowed my work as well as making it seem old fashioned to a great many critics.[15]

Wales, Landscape, and Identity

The year she spent with her aunt and uncle at Benhall was such a formative and significant a part of her life that, aged forty-eight, ill and aware that she had not long to live, she

---

14. *Ray of Darkness*, p. 12.
15. 'The Nightingale Silenced', NLW, ms 23368B (33-4).

wrote recollections of her time there for her daughter Cassandra, then a child of five. Memory, she says, 'can be *sent back* by deliberate will'[16] and the joy, happiness and freedom she experienced in that particular place remained to be drawn on when her adult self was in need of healing or being restored. For this reason she called her memoir 'The Immortal Hospital'. Benhall becomes Hill Hall in this account:

> Hill Hall is the scene where I am always at my strongest, best loved and most enthralled. Hill Hall holds my youth. When lying half awake, half teased by sleep or by my disorder or the horrible associations this disorder has brought. When burnt by sorrow and hollowed by pain, when all the misery and narrowness of that nature which is a writer's makes me writhe like a snake over my own length of Self which I have collected behind me, at moments I can still be little Margiad at Hill Hall, if I try.[17]

Evans's Romantic affiliations are clear: childhood, memory, and nature, are essential in maintaining her mental and spiritual well-being as an adult. Rhodri Hayward argues that in her 'imaginative recreation' of her childhood at Benhall, Evans 'formed a new mental environment for her failing sense of self . . . the imagined landscape of Ross on Wye could be seen as a practical mnemonic', providing in her writing 'a durable basis for her sense of identity'.[18] Interestingly, Evans equates the suffering born of her illness with 'the misery and narrowness' of a writer's nature, subscribing to romantic notions of creativity. But the main thing is that consolation can be found: it is possible to

16. 'The Immortal Hospital', NLW 23369C, 5.
17. ibid., 5.
18. Rhodri Hayward, 'Between Flesh and friendship: Margiad Evans, F. L. Golla and the Struggle for Self', forthcoming.

retrieve 'little Margiad'; those childhood days provide a bank of experience to be drawn on in later life.

In choosing her pen name, the young Englishwoman carefully laid hold of a Welsh identity for her writing: the name Evans came from her grandmother, Ann, who was thought to have a Welsh background, while 'Margiad' – perhaps more usually spelled 'Marged' – is a Welsh form of 'Margaret'. Her creativity and imagination were closely identified with the Herefordshire Border country where she spent most of her life, while she stayed at a farm in the Welsh-speaking community of Pontllyfni in Caernarfon-shire to research and write her first novel, *Country Dance*. That episode of her life becomes part of her second novel, *The Wooden Doctor*: 'The story had shifted from the English to the Welsh side of the Border. Actual information was required to continue; imagination I had not drawn upon, and it would have falsified what had been already carefully described' (134). The need to research background, self-referentially inscribed within the novel itself, functions as a signpost to her position as an 'outsider'. For while Peggy Whistler adopted a Welsh pen name, and while critics quickly labelled her as Anglo-Welsh, she was also emphatic in asserting that she was not, and never had 'posed as Welsh'.[19] On the other hand, she undoubtedly felt a psycho-logical, emotional and spiritual identification with the Border country which began (as we have seen) when she was nine years old.

As an adult, she writes in her journal of the journey home to Bridstow from Hereford:

> The chronicle of the day is lifeless, a contamination of movement and mechanical sight, until the moun-tains of Wales, indigo beyond low transparent clouds,

---

19. Quoted in Ceridwen Lloyd-Morgan, op. cit., 98.

were gathered in one splendid vision spinning backwards as we fled over the Hereford road. The ocean
which crashed about Herman Melvilles [*sic*] brain,
and the thrashing of enormous waves in his ears,
could never have meant more to him than those hills
to me, an unsealable ponderous mystery which could
drive me to frenzy and beyond if I looked at them
too long. He could express it – he was up to the glory,
but I'm mute and the hills lie on me as the water lies
on a drowned body stirring it with its own movement and dispersing it.[20]

The mountains are sublime, inspiring fear and awe, while
over-contemplation could induce frenzy and whatever mad-
ness lies beyond that. The profound effect of the landscape
on her sense of identity is compounded by the weight of
the hills and the notion of death. Self is first dissolved, then
lent movement by those same hills that seem to bury her, in
a complex image of water and drowning. The passage is
intimately bound up with what it means to be a writer, to
find expression: Melville has mastered powerful description
(and description of nature's power) whereas Evans by comparison feels herself to be mute. She cannot achieve artistic
distance or perspective as he can, she is too embedded, too
involved in it. The landscape is powerful enough to (literally)
move her, but it also seems to rob her of her power of
expression. In another journal entry made the following
year, Wales is personified as female, reclaiming land stolen
by England:

As sad, as sad and oncoming as the hills today which
put out clouds from Wales, as if she would shadow
England's stolen marches, and stake her rights with
rain and mist. The land beyond the hills means so

20. NLW, ms 23366D, 6 May 1934.

much more to me than the ground I stand on. For what I stand on only supports my flesh, but the distances uphold my heart and the hills sweep my thoughts across the sky.[21]

Again, Evans's identity is intimately and *bodily* rooted within the landscape, allowing her mind – her 'thoughts' – to expand. 'How shall I ever die out of these hills?' she asks, 'The dawn of hills, and their retreating into night. I will write a poem to them one day; for their silence drives me beyond my own'.[22] Clare Morgan, placing Evans's writing in the cultural and historical context of the 1940s, argues that Evans's Romanticism is actually Neo-Romantic. The border she inhabits 'is not that of Wales and England, but that of Peggy Whistler and Margiad Evans, a psychological, emotional and spiritual border whose aspect mirrors the prevailing cultural anxiety of a Britain seeking in its marginal spaces, rootedness.'[23]

Certainly there is a vivid contrast between the interiors and enclosed worlds that define and debilitate Evans's alter ego Arabella in *The Wooden Doctor*, and the sense of inhabiting and being part of the wider natural landscape she describes in the journals. Arabella finds it impossible 'to imagine that the foundations of [the hospital] were on earth, and that above the roof was the sky' (83), but once admitted to the ward she is told she can have tea on the balcony and: 'Directly I stepped out on the balcony I lost the feeling that I was imprisoned. . . . Why, the Infirmary owed some of its elevation to the hill on which it stood' (84). The separation between structures and institutions, and the outside natural world could not be clearer.

---

21. NLW, ms 23366D, 2 October 1935.
22. NLW, ms 23577C, 10 November 1935.
23. Clare Morgan, 'Exile and the Kingdom: Margiad Evans and the Mythic Landscape of Wales', in *Welsh Writing in English*, vol. 6, 98.

Evans's first three novels are all set in and around Ross-on-Wye, while the fourth and last, *Creed* (1936) is set in Salus (Ross) itself. Many of her short stories draw on the same landscape, while her first book of verse, *Poems from Obscurity*, was advertised as 'essentially Celtic'.[24] *Country Dance* established Evans's reputation as an Anglo-Welsh writer. In the story of the love triangle between Ann Goodman (child of an English father and a Welsh mother), Gabriel Ford the Englishman, and Evan ap Evans the Welshman, is 'represented the entire history of the Border. . . . Wales against England – and the victory goes to Wales; like Evan ap Evans the awakened Celt cries: "Cymru am byth!" with every word she writes'.[25] These are Margiad Evans's own 'editorial' comments framing Ann Goodman's journal, a nineteenth-century manuscript she purports to find and presents to her readers – in an eighteenth-century literary tradition. When *The Wooden Doctor* came out the following year, the *Daily Herald* said 'something new and surprising has come out of Wales' while the *Times Literary Supplement* said 'There is an uncompromising harshness about Miss Margiad Evans's new story "The Wooden Doctor" . . . born perhaps of the Welsh hill country, which was also the background of her earlier book, "Country Dance".[26] Rightly or wrongly, the link between writer and Wales was firmly established in critics' minds.

Literary Context

Margiad Evans published novels, short stories, and poetry, as well as two other works: *Autobiography* (1943), which as

---

24. *Wales*, February-March 1948.
25. *Country Dance*, (1978) London: John Calder, 95.
26. *TLS*, 23 March 1933, 198.

we have seen is not autobiography in a conventional sense, and *A Ray of Darkness* (1952) describing the epilepsy which marked her later years. *The Welsh Review* published a number of her poems, *Life and Letters Today* accepted several of her essays, and she made broadcasts for the Welsh Home Service. Her writing has been compared to that of D. H. Lawrence, Emily Bronte, Richard Jeffries, John Cowper Powys and his brother Llewelyn, while Idris Parry, dwelling on the visionary aspects of her writing, makes a connection with the mystic Henry Vaughan.[27]

Although she never met the celebrated Welsh writer Kate Roberts, Evans admired her work and the respect was mutual. The two corresponded for some years after Evans reviewed a collection of Kate Roberts's short stories which had been translated into English, *A Summer's Day* (1946), in *Life and Letters Today*.[28] They had much in common, not least the distinction of being 'in danger of being marginalised by English critics, especially since they chose to write about what they knew best, rather than what might be acceptable or fashionable'.[29] Themes of childhood, memory, old age, and the vicissitudes of rural life for working women, together with a strong sense of place – scenes which might be circumscribed in location but 'are wide in inference'[30] are also common to both writers. Kate Roberts's stories, including her novels *Feet In Chains* (1936) and *The Living Sleep* (1956), are set in the quarrying districts of Caernarfonshire, places Evans knew from writing and researching *Country Dance*.

Evans was not the first woman writer to be accused of narrow horizons, and in the company of others such as

---

27. Idris Parry, 'Margiad Evans', *Silence Speaks* (1988) Manchester: Carcanet, 315.
28. November 1946.
29. Ceridwen Lloyd-Morgan, op.cit., 107.
30. ibid 107.

Jane Austen and Kate Roberts, there is no need to defend
her from such charges. She was honoured by the Welsh
Committee of the Arts Council with an award for *A Candle
Ahead* – her second volume of poems which had come out
in 1956 – an award which *The Times* reported a week before
she died, on her 49th birthday, 17 March 1958.

TO THE WOODEN DOCTOR

O clair de la lune,
Mon ami Pierrot,
Prête moi ta plume
Pour écrire un mot.
Ma chandelle est morte,
Je n'ai plus de feu,
Ouvre moi ta porte
Pour l'amour de Dieu.

PRINCIPAL CHARACTERS

JOHN FLAHERTY—An Irish doctor.
JULIAN MANNEL—All Englishman.
OLIVER AUSTEN.
JEANNE-MARIE DESSIER—The Directrice of the
   Cours Saint-Louis.
ARABELLA WARDEN ⎫ —sisters
ESTHER WARDEN   ⎭

All characters in this book are purely imaginary.

M.E.

Prelude

We moved into our house in nineteen twenty-one when I was twelve and my sister Esther nine.

For a year we had been living with an aunt in the same neighbourhood, hardly half a mile away. Our father was with us, but I do not remember that we saw him often. Our mother was with her people. Our elder sister went to boarding school; she appeared in the holidays, very tall and wearing beads. Her short crop had been allowed to grow into soft curls on her neck and her breast was no longer flat. We asked her if she did not find this uncomfortable? She said not in the least. She refused to bathe with us.

Esther and I never cleaned our teeth. We were always dirty and untidy. Across our high, bony foreheads our hair fell in unbrushed strings; our legs were so long and skinny, our bodies so slight, that we looked like insects.

Esther's short, straight nose was my father's, as were her beautiful sensual lips. My nose turned up, and my mouth was like a gash. I had brown hair as thick as a mat. When it was washed it took three hours to dry.

Our relations said Catherine was beautiful, and Esther promised well in spite of her deplorable tendency to make the worst of herself; but I should always be plain. What hair! Sometimes they curled it and then it flew about worse than ever. I tried to pull some of it out by the roots but the intense pain made me desist.

My aunt sent us to school at Salus. We were always late because we dawdled on the way eating the biscuits she had given us for lunch, playing with the dogs in the road, or searching the hedges and banks for birds' nests. Our egg collection was very large and carefully classified. We never took more than one egg from a nest.

If we now possessed one half the knowledge of birds and their breeding haunts that we practised then we should be considered distinguished naturalists.

We did not so much dislike school as disregard it. I was quite amenable, but Esther refused to learn anything. In due course, as she grew too old to remain in the kinder-garten, they moved her up, and she sat as she had done before, silent and inattentive. She was composing ghost stories which she related during break. For this she was nearly expelled.

She could not read, nor did she want to learn, because I always read to her.

At twelve o'clock we fled.

My cousins discovered that she could not tell the time. They made no attempt to teach her, but they did expose her ignorance whenever possible.

'Never mind, we'll sell our red egg for a hundred pounds and go away,' she said. This red egg was a pullet's, painted and hidden for us to find. The child's imagination proved stronger than the expert's lore: we searched through all our books and found no mention of a red egg. Esther said con-tentedly:

'It is very, very rare indeed.'

We knew that our parents had bought a house. Our aunt took us to call on the tenant. She sat on a green and gold striped sofa and a green parakeet sidled up her shoulder. The woman's long silk-covered legs, contrasting strangely with our brown shins and our aunt's stumps, ended in green shoes. Her face was a flower drooping from a dry stalk, a strange, painted flower, or a mask.

A huge French motto hung over the fireplace. While we

were sitting there I tried to read it, but the verbs 'avoir' and 'être' were not contained in it, at least not as I had met them.

The next time we went we were alone, the tenant had left, and all the rooms were empty.

The grass had grown like a hayfield; a red chestnut-tree shed blossoms in a circle, there were buds on the wisteria and where the twisted branches planted themselves round the veranda pillars we found a snug place to put the bull-finch's egg that we were carrying, while we explored the garden and the sheds.

Suddenly the rain showered on us. We ran to shelter in the veranda. Esther blew the egg on the red tiles. I peered through the glass door into the long bare room where we had sat near the fantastic, bedizened lady.

I can still see it now, though with an effort, as it was then. I can still see it, if I look behind years and many noises, empty and silent. I can almost see it as it will be again when we are gone, painted a strange colour, harbouring another family; but that is harder.

A month later we moved in. Esther and I were given a room together; what lack of bedrooms entailed we would have chosen. Our beds stood side by side. As we were un-dressing she told me that I should soon be like Catherine. I looked down at myself angrily, noticing faint curves of flesh.

A servant had warned me that I would soon experience other changes. I awaited with fearful curiosity.

I began to read more and faster.

'Oh, do come out and leave that book,' was Esther's constant urgent cry.

I usually did, but I was aware that I had entered into a new region where as yet she could not follow me.

We discovered the country behind our house to be alto-gether new to us, and inevitably forsook many corners where we had played the ground bare. The extra mile to school procured us bicycles. I do not know whether the machines had anything to do with it, but our long lean growth advanced rapidly towards absurdity. In the winter Esther had a bad fall. She cut her knee so severely that our mother sent for the doctor.

Esther sat in the armchair in the dining-room, her injured leg lying out before her, stiff on a stool. She did not cry until the doctor insisted that she should laugh, and then she burst into loud wails. Her eyes swelled; tears beaded the front of her dress.

The doctor, an elderly man who lacked self-control, stammered and used jerky gestures to illumine his inarticulation. He said she must be inoculated against tetanus. His mouth bubbled as he jabbered. In the evening he returned with his assistant.

I had been sent to the kitchen. I heard the doctor stuttering and shouting. Esther screamed terribly, everyone expostulated. Then a voice that was strange said something I could not hear. That gentle decisive tone reduced the hubbub to a murmur, and Esther did not cry out again.

*   *   *

One morning at school I suddenly began to feel very cold. I shuddered till my desk rattled and my teeth chattered. In the dinner hour I went home for I knew I was going to be ill.

My mother put me to bed. The cold sheets were awful. She brought me a hot-water bottle, and, gripping it, I fell asleep.

I woke up in scorching fever. My mother, standing at the foot of the bed, looked strange to me, far away and indistinctly distorted. The room seemed enormous; the walls wavered in and out as though they were paper, the floor heaved.

As I turned my head I saw a man beside me. I asked him:
'Why does mother's face look so queer?'
'Because ye aren't very well.'
'Are you the doctor?'
'I am.'
'What is your name?'
'Flaherty. What's yours?'
'Arabella. I'm so hot. Feel my hands.'
'Yes. Lie still. I want to sound ye'er chest.'
'May I listen?'
'No, don't talk.'

I stared at the thoughtful face bent above me. I had never seen him before. He unbuttoned my nightgown, pushed it open. My chest was glistening. As the stethoscope moved I suddenly knew terror, not of him not his machine – no, indeed – but of a dreadful, indescribable nightmare, a nightmare that came to us when we were wide-eyed, a nightmare that Esther shared with me and which we spoke about to each other and to nobody else. Everything glided smoothly, swiftly, flowing like the road beneath a car, then, oh, awful, oh, horror – chaos, weltering, tangled confusion.

The room whirled and straightened for its spinning rush; my mother vanished into a void; I saw the doctor at the end of a long, long tunnel and sobbed at what was coming. From infinite distance he stretched out his hand, sliding it between my head and the pillow, and gathered my hair from my burning face. In the same moment the room swung back into focus. His touch had cheated the terror. 'My head does ache!'

He twisted my hair to keep it back: 'Shall I cut off ye'er beautiful hair?

'Do you *like* it?'

'I do; it's a rope that would hang an elephant.'

This was my first meeting with the Wooden Doctor.

He was an Irishman of about forty, and unmarried. A year later he bought the practice and a sombre brown stone house just outside Salus. Every day he drove past our school, and if I saw him I waved.

Everybody discussed his inevitable marriage. Whom would he choose? But he did not marry.

*   *   *

In our home there was no peace. My father did more than drink occasionally; he was an habitual and incurable drunkard. No word was ever more accurately or deservedly applied; no family was ever rendered more miserable by its justice.

While we were young our mother would have made efforts to shield us from this knowledge, but her attempts were unsuccessful, partly because our father, roaming the house wildly, would never confine himself to one room, and partly because our perceptions were really abnormally acute.

Twenty years of marriage had done no more than confirm her suspicions; even to the end she believed that half his outbursts were due to illness; I can hardly remember a time when we did not know what he was. He bewildered her.

We grew up accepting him at first with terror and disgust, finally with bitter resignation. We have heard our mother called by names that would have shamed a harlot, not below the breath, but as one might sing praises. We have stood shivering behind bolted doors with our hands over our ears that we might not hear him scream of the horrors that he saw, and shut our eyes to those that were not delirious fancy.

Sometimes for our own sake and his own we have wished him dead, drowned, buried, or for ourselves that freedom.

As we grew older there was less violence, and by that time very little could touch us. Is there not proof, here on this paper, written in this hand, that I for one have achieved indifference? If there should appear a bitter line here and again, it is stale, a mood from the past that rose in invocation, and dispersed before the end of the sentence. There is no need to dwell on this. Where we had feared and hated we now pitied and despised: our father's attitude reacted to the change. His health gave way, he became quieter in his degradation, in his ruin more complete. Then he was more terrible than ever before, with a look in his eyes that might well lead one to suspect his sanity. Usually he was out all day; late at night he would return, and if he were not always drunk, at least he was seldom, very seldom sober.

The lamps would be turned low, the guard put over the embers, but even with these precautions one of us would always sit up to make sure he did not set fire to the house. Often we had to look outside for him with a lantern.

There was an old grandfather clock in the hall which, however late or fuddled his entry, he never failed to wind before he went upstairs to bed. He would wrench at the chain as though to tear it out, and by some fault in the works, the harsh grinding ended in a clear, sweet chime. He never forgot it.

The forbearance of our mother was such that once I asked her:

'Do you still care for him?'

'Do you want the truth?'

'Yes.'

'I hate him.'

We had no friends: his behaviour alienated all our neigh-bours. In fairness I add that the addition of their friendship would have meant very little to any of us, and we were too poor to entertain.

One and all, year in, year out, as we grew up or old, we nursed the prospect of escape. We quarrelled among our-selves; fretted, isolated by our eccentricities, we sharpened our claws in one another's flesh. Our home among the quiet fields became a cage of savagery.

PART ONE

Part One

One night in October when I was sixteen, I was awake long after my family slept. I had been packing, for next day I was going to La Touraine as a pupil teacher. I had put out the candle and sat on the closed trunk looking out of the window at the sheep in the field below, wandering about in the moonlight. For hours I heard no sound other than the wind in the holly-tree, till very early in the morning my father came up the lane.

It was one of those times when he could not find his way through the gate; even when held at arm's-length from the window, a candle was too faint and high a light to guide him.

I went out. If the house were cold in those small still hours, how bitterly breathed the little wind outside that only stirred the leaves! I moved so quietly, opened the door so stealthily, that no sleeper could have heard me, yet when we returned minutes later my mother was standing in the kitchen with a lamp in her hand.

She did not speak; after one glance she turned it low and I blew out the lantern that we might not see. One gleam shone still upon her face and his, and mine reflected in a mirror until I bent my head.

He had fallen on a chair; dead leaves clung to his clothes, which were muddy from lying in the lane.

'Go to bed,' said my mother, warning and imploring.

My father suddenly screamed. What happened then was, as always, like a play which must be acted as it was written, words and gestures repeated, actors inscrutably elected, audience as God ordained it.

High heaven, but, played by such a ghastly clown! It was horrible! Desperately, wearily, sternly, with all her heart my mother cried:

'See the horrors of a drunken man!'

I looked for all my life.

Later still, when I thought him sleeping, he came out of his room into the passage. The yellow light of his wavering candle shone under our door, and I sprang to lock it. As he walked he muttered and coughed until it seemed that he must split his lungs, and called for us. No power on earth would have made me go to him.

The next day I was too ill to travel, and the doctor came. All that I craved, all the things existence had so far denied me, I found in him, and in him only. About him there was always an air of gentle wisdom, and though many people have said that gentleness was not his, I never failed to find it. Perhaps they had not searched, for it lay beneath a casual manner and seldom appeared in speech. His voice, of which he was particularly sparing, had great charm for me. If I were sad his presence brought me comfort; if happy, sympathy; if disturbed, peace.

My mother told him of the scene we had passed through. She blamed my father for my illness. He listened in silence, his eyes fixed thoughtfully on a jar of flowers, and when she had finished, crossed the room and, sitting on the bed, smiled down at me. Neither then nor at any time in my hearing, did he pronounce any opinion of my father.

I had been in pain – it was over: I had longed for him – he was there. My bare arm lay along my side. His hand rested on it.

After he had gone I slept till midnight, when a furious gale awoke me. The house shook; it seemed as though demons were tearing at the walls, the branches were flung against the panes, the rain poured.

Autumn, wild, angry, tumultuous, riotous autumn; kill-ing, cleansing, ushering autumn, stripped of the gorgeous colours and the placid fruits, undimmed by hazy bonfire smoke, unseen but heard and felt in bitter storm alone at black midnight.

Sheltered from the frenzied uproar without, the lamp upon the table by my bed burned steadily without a flicker.

*   *   *

Mademoiselle Dessier, directrice du Cours Saint-Louis.

She met us at the station. In the train my mother and I had been disputing; as the directrice approached we drew together. Powder clung to her face and neck, flat curls were smarmed on her cheeks. She had eyes like aquamarines, and enormously thick black brows. She shook hands with my mother rather ceremoniously, and turned to me with a smile:

'Vous êtes grande, Mademoiselle Arabelle; c'est déjà quelquechose.'

She added that several of my pupils would be older than myself, 'et d'une type très avancée.'

She was pleased when I showed her I had pinned up my hair. I had cut it almost to my shoulders.

We walked through the town to the school.

Passing the church the directrice demanded:

'Vous êtes Protestante, sans doute?'

I found it difficult to define my beliefs so suddenly, and my answer was purely formal rather than truly informative.

'Yes, mademoiselle.'

She nodded:

'It is all one,' she replied indifferently. In her letters she had never touched upon this point, though she had put

several searching questions touching my family and con-
nections.

Our walk was short. The Cours Saint-Louis stood back
from the road, facing a convent orphanage a little way out
of the town. A quiet street led up to it, but it was the last
house, and a hundred yards farther up the yellow road the
lamp-posts ceased where trees began: a rise in the ground
hid the country beyond.

The school in reality was a great deal smaller than the
photographs had led us to expect. Somewhere in Moras
there must have been a cunning photographer. But it was
a beautiful house, a small château, white with regularly
placed windows; they were all shut. Over the door, at
the top of a wide flight of steps flanked by carved stone
balustrades, was a strip of old stained-glass showing the
head of Agnès Sorel surrounded by decorously skipping
lambs. Her white face and yellow hair stood out from the
ruby-red background. In the castle on the hill she was
buried.

A short, straight drive rose to this stately entrance, on
either side of which stood giant acacias. Beneath them among
the long grass and the fallen leaves bloomed thousands of
tiny cyclamen.

It appeared that Mademoiselle la directrice shared her
responsibilities with a friend whose existence was completely unsuspected by us until we were introduced. Her
name was Baschet. Short, and very fat, she seemed much
older than the directrice, who was tall and thin. The one
seemed a withered exotic, the other an expanded nurse. A
strange couple.

We had an omelet, followed by larks on toast, to eat. I
loathed the tiny carcasses. They came up from the basement kitchen on a wooden lift. Mademoiselle Baschet ate
hers with gusto, but the directrice, holding the twiggy

bones delicately in her long fingers, talked incessantly and restlessly to my mother; my knowledge of French being more grammatical than colloquial, I could not understand very much of their conversation. Mademoiselle Baschet saw this. She patted my hand; hers were greasy.

'You will soon learn. Meanwhile, we all understand music. As we have finished, I will play to you.'

'My friend is an accomplished musician,' remarked the directrice.

Mademoiselle Baschet chose the Pastoral Symphony, which she seemed to know by heart. My mother was a great lover of Beethoven, and as such sat in horror-stricken silence while the music proceeded according to French provincial standards, rapidly, loudly, and easily. The performer kept her foot on the pedal the whole time. When at the end she unclamped it, I noticed that a bright patch had been worn on the dirty brass; by contrast the damper pedal appeared unused. The keys were filthy. The directrice inquired blandly:

'Was it not beautiful?'

I was obliged to answer, for my mother could find nothing to say.

The directrice rang a bell. The girl who answered it entered the great double doors soundlessly; she wore list slippers, which glided over the polished floor, and a dark cotton frock. Her eyes glittered with laughter and curiosity.

'Rose, ask Mademoiselle Mimi Maréchal to come here.'

Rose cast a rapid glance at the directrice. She crossed the room quickly, bending her knees sinuously. Pushing a panel aside, she thrust her head through the aperture and cried loudly:

'Mimi Maréchal au salon!'

The babel of a turbulent class ceased. The directrice bent her gaze upon the floor, her underlip protruding. Mademoiselle Baschet reproved the servant, waggling her finger at the fault. Nevertheless, it was not towards her, but to the directrice Rose flung the half merry, half defiant look with which she left the room.

'She is a Parisienne, and very impudent.'

'She has no manners, certainly,' added Mademoiselle Baschet.

My mother had smiled at the sight of the girl's beauty.

Mimi Maréchal appeared. She was thus the first pupil that I met. Mademoiselle Baschet loved her for her prowess at the piano, and indeed she could play faster than any girl in the town. This promising student was presented with pride, and, standing demurely before my mother, put her hands behind her back as they were made to do in class when reciting: after a moment or two she laughed and threw back her long golden plaits which reached to her knees.

'She is of very good family,' observed the directrice.

'And very good and very clever herself,' continued Mademoiselle Baschet, gently pushing Mimi towards the piano. 'Play a little, my child.'

'Voyons, Suzanne, you are spoiling the child! She must return to her work.'

With a little grimace Mimi went.

The directrice walked with me in the grounds that afternoon while my mother rested. She had wrapped herself in a lace shawl. She showed me the shrubbery, where the dead leaves lay lightly on the springing cyclamen, and the vegetable garden.

'We have salad every day.'

Flowers there were none in this enclosure of utility but a single row of frost-smitten carnations where one scarlet blossom still bloomed. She gave it to me, and I did not know what to do with it.

A woman in a white coif was cutting chicory.

'Eugénie,' said the directrice.

The woman raised her head, looking sharply at me; she had a red, kind, yet peevish face which wore always an expression of fretful trouble not without humour. She was the cook.

'Bon jour, Mam'selle.'

'Bon jour,' I answered, and as we left her she bent over her work again, murmuring endlessly, wearily:

'Mon dieu, mon dieu, mon dieu.' It was her habit.

At the back of the house the directrice pointed out the patch under two great trees where the girls played. The ground was worn smooth by their feet, stamped hard in nimble *cache-cache-courir* in agile *marelle,* and nimble *un deux trois.*

There were two swings. A new classroom with ground glass windows opened on the playground. 'Here,' said the directrice, 'the English studies were pursued.'

On one step a small sandy cat sat sunning itself. I stretched out my hand towards it, but she caught at my wrist:

'Do not touch him, he is wicked!' And the cat, waking in a moment from sleepy content to tigerish ferocity, pathetic and terrible in so tiny a creature, sprang furiously at me so that I gave way before the unnatural onslaught, dismayed at those distended yellow eyes, those unsheathed curving claws.

The directrice watched. She repeated colourlessly:

'Il est méchant.'

*   *   *

My mother stayed only one night at the Cours Saint-Louis because she was afraid to leave my father.

We had a little room together over the front porch. Very early in the morning Rose brought her some coffee and before it was light she had dressed. I lay in bed watching her put on her clothes. It had frozen in the night; the air was icy, colder than I had ever known it at home.

She was quick: when coming to me she bent down to kiss me and whisper good-bye; weakly, rebelliously and fearfully I was crying.

'I hate it, mother!'

'It won't be long till Easter.'

Afterwards she told me the place had filled her with the same dislike and distrust that from then onwards I could not repress. As she left me I knew she was going away uneasy.

I saw her standing in the drive talking to the directrice. Frost had jammed the window-fastening, but I tore it open, leaning out in my nightgown to wave and call to her.

She knew to what she was returning; I thought it preferable to the directrice. She gave me no cause to change that opinion.

My mother went. It was a mistake.

The directrice sent two girls to help me unpack and show me where I was to sleep. Their names were Andrée and Yvonne, and they were the head girls. Both were older than myself. They had been given special permission to call me by my Christian name, which they appeared to consider was 'Mees,' 'Arabella' being my nom-de-famille.

I slept in a dormitory with fourteen others. My bed had a screen round it.

After we had put the clothes in a cupboard we went down to breakfast. The directrice sat at the top of one long table, her arms and legs crossed, leaning her weight forward, her head level. She wore a hideous salmon-pink woollen coat, and diamond ear-rings. I counted only three institutrices. They all looked cold and sulky, and not more than half awake. The boarders kept their eyes fixed on their plates. A very stout girl sat opposite me. I heard them call her Pierrette.

The directrice gave a swift thanksgiving and we all got up. A red-headed institutrice, folding her lips in a thin line, shepherded the pupils from the room. Almost immediately three pianos were heard.

The directrice took me through a high, grey-walled room with a stone floor. 'This is where you sit in the evenings.' She opened a glass door. We stood at the head of a flight of steps and from this point of vantage she introduced me to the girls. Strangely, curiously, we looked at one another. We did not know what to say, and perfunctorily smiling, went, all of us, about our own business.

*   *   *

From the beginning I hated it all. A month or so before I went to the Cours Saint-Louis my eyes had begun to fail, and my first view of France was through glasses. It was quite sudden, and the oculist attributed it to excessive blackboard study during my preparation for School Certificate. He stressed the necessity for good light. Warned as the directrice had been of this, she allotted me a desk in the corner away from the single light; indeed, it was no more than justice for we all suffered alike.

Very often during the long study hours in the dark evenings, a pupil put away her pen and, closing her eyes, leaned her head on her hand. From her estrade the watchful institutrice in charge would demand the reason for this idleness:

'Why have you stopped working, you down there?'

'Mademoiselle, my eyes hurt.'

If it were Mademoiselle Portier the mathematician, or Mademoiselle Dupont the peasant, this excuse provoked an outburst of furious denunciation which, beginning in a hissing whisper, culminated perhaps ten minutes later in shrieks of abuse. Then the institutrice, striding the room, flourished her arms in wide gestures, her eyes flashed, and her one object seemed to be the utter annihilation of her victim, who, I observed, as the noise increased, the diatribe waxed, and the institutrice paused before delivering the ultimate blow, regained her composure completely, and resumed both her work and her official posture with stolid indifference.

Neither the fiery Portier nor the cruel Dupont could draw a tear.

With Monsieur le professeur de littérature – whose title in full delighted me – they were plentiful as drops in a fountain and no more unexpected. He was an elderly man. Grey of hair and clothing, deliberate of speech, golden of voice, who came every other day to take the two upper classes. As part of my studies I was obliged to follow the course. I found it hard; usually he read very fast; frequently, when moved, he became unintelligible to me. Then, seeing that I was plodding despairingly in his wake, he would gently encourage me:

'Suivez donc, Mees Arabella, suivez donc.'

For two minutes he would be quite coherent, till, forgetting anything so insignificant as myself in the glory of French literature, he would set off once more, the entire class pursuing him as best they might with a great fluttering of pages and heaving of gusty sighs.

There were many, many commonplace words I could not understand, and for these no explanations were given, even if I had had the time to ask for them, but occasionally the professor lit upon a colourful word or phrase which, being unusual or idiomatic, touched his imagination, and induced him to give me the meaning in dumb show, as he had no knowledge of English.

Once he chose 'mal de mer.' I understood it very well, because it was literal, and I sat back prepared to enjoy thoroughly monsieur's rendering of it.

He arose, and stood upon his chair, which, together with the height of the estrade, raised him to within a few inches of the ceiling. Clasping his hands over his diaphragm he imitated in mime the sufferings which every landsman anticipates. As the professor reached the climax the glass door opened on the directrice whom he did not appear to see. She stood silently regarding the performance. Descending, she caught his eye. He observed blandly:

'That was well done?'

'Very well done.'

Turning her head towards him she fixed her eyes on him in so wanton a glance that I was startled. It did not invite, rather it accepted, amorousness. She was laughing, her mouth curved upwards towards the high prominent cheek-bones.

The professor was married. It was murmured among the older girls that previous to choosing his wife he had asked the directrice; the look she had given him, her laughter, and the softened features expressed nothing so conventional. The professor was not often so lively; his moods varied, but he was, as a rule, strict, and then all heads were bent before him.

He did not, as Portier, lean across his desk, clench his hands and hurl invective; he did not, as Dupont, wet his lips and crush the culprit in a wild hysterical outburst. Severely he selected a candidate for his displeasure, which never violent, had the capacity for rousing the emotions. In spite of this it must have been that the fear he evoked was of a very transitory nature as his lessons were never prepared. Struck dumb in their ignorance, girl after girl rose in her place quite unable to recite a line, and after a few stumbling attempts wept abundantly and sat down. The professor lectured, she promised to do better, and so they went on.

One proved the exception: Ginette le Guay spoke with the accent of the midi, and in her deep, resonant tones she could, when she liked, recite verse. She never shed a tear; she stared monsieur out of countenance; she enchanted him with her magnificent black eyes and delighted his heart with spirited renderings of his favourite passages. Her undoubted brilliance, her laziness, her charm, and her very great beauty provoked and beguiled us all. She had at school a younger sister, Louise, who shared her indolence; possessing an even sharper wit, she lacked Ginette's fascination; she defied the whole staff, not, however, at all to her discomfiture.

We used to see this family at church on Sundays with their parents. There were about a dozen, all wearing black and white check coats, from Ginette to the youngest, of all sizes, and apparently all one sex: at least, there was no distinction in garb and very little in countenance. They were very poor.

It seems to me that there were very few remarkable personalities among the girls. Some were hearty, but not a few had comical or threatening ailments. Thérèse coughed all day and night; the cold made Pierrette sick; Renée cried in bed.

Once I went to her; we had to whisper because if Mademoiselle Michelet had heard she would have complained to the directrice.

'Pourquoi pleurez-vous, Renée?'

'Pour Maman.'

'Elle est loin?'

'Elle est morte.'

*   *   *

We had not enough to eat.

After the first two weeks the intense cold deepened day by day. Without adequate heating in that stone house, we suffered horribly, at once shivering and stifling for fresh air. The windows were always shut. One night in desperation I secretly rose and opened one. I chose the farthest away from Michelet's corner, and when I saw a light shine through her white shroud-like curtains I knew she had heard me. She demanded: 'What are you doing?' poking her head out and rubbing her eyes fretfully.

'I feel sick. I want some air.'

'Shut it.'

The head withdrew, and the light was extinguished.

In the morning she complained bitterly of the draught. The directrice ordered me to leave the windows alone.

Mademoiselle Michelet was the oldest institutrice; she was a small, dark, sharp woman who smiled spitefully and showed long teeth green at the roots. Her eyelids were inflamed for want of sleep – she could not sleep. She had a certain pathos and, although she frequently lost her temper, she did not go to the lengths of Mesdemoiselles Portier and Dupont.

Aline Portier, red-haired and implacable, taught mathematics with passion, and history with cool precision that demanded a concentration from the girls seldom accorded to anyone but the directrice. In moments of tranquillity she was dignified, in a rage, nothing short of demented.

Marie Dupont, round-faced and red-cheeked, not a bone in her skull showing through the flesh, short and gross, gave a deceptive impression of good humour. In reality she was irritable and very often cruel. Hysteria ravaged her, and passed, leaving marks on all but herself. Her domain was the lower school where she was hated. When she conducted the older boarders for a walk or evening study, she used with a peasant's cunning to gain their favour by a ridiculous camaraderie. She was very young and among them she was popular.

After dinner, when it was dusk, and we all sat in our stony 'recreation' room waiting for bed, the three institutrices would draw their chairs together so that their knees touched, talking and laughing so loudly, waving their arms in such emphatic gestures, that they were usually possessors of half the room before very long, while the rest crowded as far away from them as possible. In the high room those dreadful falsetto-shrieks of laughter echoed shrill and toneless, and the institutrices huddled like birds on a perch, tore at the air as though theirs were not hands but claws. Laugh away, yelling macaws.

*   *   *

Michelet's voice woke us every morning.

'Levez vous, mes enfants!'

The girls got up, put on their dressing-gowns, turned back their beds, and went up to the top storey to the wash-room. Their dresses hung from pegs outside, their petticoats, bloomers and stays festooned the bed railings. They were never allowed to bath.

The directrice permitted me to stay in bed until the others had finished. Michelet called me:

'Vous pouvez monter.'

And I mounted to the wash-room and the row of tin basins.

A monotonous prayer began and ended our day; it lasted fully seven minutes and I remember only one phrase because of the action that accompanied it. Hitting themselves rhythmically upon the breast-bone, everyone proclaimed:

'C'est ma faute, c'est ma faute, c'est ma trés grande faute.'

Always this mysterious fault remained unexplained and isolated in a hum of words.

Besides these devotions the girls prayed aloud as they dressed and undressed, one leading and the others answering as they pulled on their stockings or let out the strings of their stays.

Pierrette, swaddled in many layers of undergarments, usually took the solo, and was still droning away when Mademoiselle put out the light and drew the white curtains round her bed. Grace was repeated before meals by the youngest pupil, aged five; the directrice stood behind him and guided his hand in the sign of the cross. Everybody adored him, particularly Andrée and Yvonne, who watched him tenderly. 'Au nom du Père, au nom du Fils, au nom du Saint-Esprit.'

Then the directrice gave him little sweet biscuits shaped like hazel nuts. Our meals were simple to starvation and brief. The Cours Saint-Louis having a greater proportion of day-girls than boarders, there were only two long tables in the salle à manger, plentifully supplied with diners but little dinner.

Mademoiselle la directrice and Mademoiselle Baschet had theirs served apart in their own rooms.

At the midday meal the directrice invariably mixed a salad. When we had finished we washed our spoons and forks in bowls carried round by Rose, and wiped them on our dinner napkins. The directrice presided over each dish; before we had well begun to eat she would demand:

'Personne ne veut plus?'

Occasionally, if we had gobbled, we were able to ask for more. Otherwise the food was whisked away leaving us very hungry. As we paid for satisfaction with indigestion, we were careful not to bolt our food every day, but there was one hungry girl, Anne-Marie Dupuis, who, having a naturally enormous appetite, exercised her jaws so expediently that she was always ready to stay the hovering dish, with the result that she suffered frequently from a violent pain when the time-table demanded that she should exercise that portion of her head less agile than her mouth – her brain. There were no separate chairs in the classes, and three or four girls had to share the same bench. Unfortunately for me, Anne-Marie was my immediate neighbour; when she began to rock to and fro in agony the bench rocked with her, and my work suffered greatly in consequence.

My mother had arranged for me to be treated as an institutrice, expecting that I should have more freedom and some consideration. The former, a thing unknown at the Cours Saint-Louis, I hardly expected; the latter was accorded to me in the form of a screen round my bed, and during the first fortnight, two pieces of toast with my chocolate in the mornings.

I could also have a bath once a week supposing it did not inconvenience me to carry it up four flights from the basement kitchen to the attic, in several cans. An old tin bath abandoned as junk by the directrice just as she dispensed with its use as superfluous, was placed at my disposal. I used folded brown paper for a bath mat, and made a pathway in the dust to the door. The window was choked with cobwebs.

These customs were privileges; one other there was attendant on my position as a young Englishwoman – that I should be, by pupils and teachers alike, left severely alone.

*   *   *

Twice a week – on Thursdays and Sundays – we were taken for a long walk in the country. The day-girls went with us and one institutrice. Outside the town the girls were free to walk as they liked. They straggled so far ahead that the voice of authority had to strain to make itself heard.

The grey, flat roads ran dully between fields of grapes. Sometimes, but not often, we went to the forest. The rumour that the boars it harboured were savage, and even the trees themselves, excited me, raised my spirits above the stupid level that I cultivated. The forest made me miserable because it also enlivened me.

We returned to school through Beaulieu. In the dusk it looked a lonely, mean little town with its fly-blown windows and its tall tower. I saw a very tall man whom I felt sure was English; I fancied that he stared at me as though he had seen me before, but his face was quite strange to me . . .

I did wish the directrice would allow me to go out alone. I wanted to explore Laroche. But if I wanted to post a letter an institutrice walked with me the hundred yards to the pillar-box.

My English classes were a success; at first, before she was satisfied that I could maintain authority and make myself understood, the directrice used to sit beside me: after a week or so she left me alone.

One day, as the girls were reading their exercises aloud, Rose burst in at the glass door, her hair in curlers half hidden under a coloured cap, her eyes dancing. She planted herself in front of the estrade, her hands spread on her hips, balancing on her heels. I knew her tendency to practical jokes, and disorder was already breaking out. I asked her bluntly what she wanted. She explained volubly:

'Mademoiselle la directrice has sent me to ask you to go at once to the salon, Mees Arabelle.'

'Why?'

'Why? How should I know?'

'Go and ask Mademoiselle la directrice who will occupy themselves with my class while I am away.'

'Moi alors.'

She actually prepared to mount the estrade. A wave of laughter threatened to capsize my authority; with a glare, and two sharp raps on the desk I righted it, at the same time turning my shoulder towards the impudent domestic. She plucked at my arm.

'I assure you, mees, the directrice desires your presence in the salon immediately.'

Unconvinced, I told her to go away, and as she vehemently protested the truth of her assertion, and the seriousness of her errand, the panel above my head slid back. Mademoiselle Baschet smiled and beckoned. Rose evidently had an authentic message; I hesitated no longer, glad as I was of any event, however trivial, to break the monotonous routine.

Outside the salon doors I paused for a moment. Mademoiselle Baschet was playing the piano, as was her custom, with her foot rooted to the pedal, but above the outraged instrument I could hear the directrice's high laughter, and a man's voice in conversation.

I opened the door. The directrice stood with her back to me, her head tilted up, in lively conversation, and a very tall young man looked down at her. I had seen him before in Beaulieu. Mademoiselle Baschet took her hands off the keys.

'Jeanne-Marie – Arabelle.'

The directrice turned, and taking me affectionately by the shoulder, introduced us somewhat incoherently.

'Bon jour, monsieur.'

'Bon jour, mademoiselle.'

Simultaneously we looked to the directrice for an explanation. She laughed again at our inquiring expressions – I hated her when she laughed, her face fell to pieces – and the diamonds in her ears flashed beneath her black hair. She was dressed very tidily. Usually her costume was striking, one garment at variance with another and the colours frankly at war, but today she had cast off the salmon-pink woollen coat, the white silk scarf, the blue skirt and purple list slippers in favour of a black gown. It suited her.

Her friend had discarded the dirty grey shawl in which she shrouded her shoulders.

The directrice's amusement puzzled me. She stood silently regarding us, a tinge of malice in her smile. We spoke together:

'Pourquoi—', I began with difficulty.

'Do you teach here – est-ce que vous êtes une institutrice?' he broke in.

'Oui – I mean, yes. You're English, aren't you?'

'Of course. Are you?'

'Yes. Oh, why didn't they tell us!'

We exchanged names. His was Julian Mannel.

'Mademoiselle Baschet teaches me to play the piano,' he said. .

'Oh, the Pastoral Symphony?'

'No, I can't play well enough to tackle that yet. Mimi can.'

'Mimi Maréchal?'

'Yes. You know her? I live with the Maréchals. Supposed to be learning French, only I'm afraid I still prefer to talk English.'

'That's awkward because I'm the only other English person in the town. Till just now I thought there wasn't another.'

He stared.

'I say, and you're quite young, aren't you – for a mistress, I mean? I saw you arriving with your mother – you had a yellow jersey. I was looking over the castle wall. The Maréchals live close to the castle, on top of the hill and we see every-thing.'

'I see nothing. Once Mademoiselle caught me looking over the garden wall counting the widows, and she was furious.'

'What a shame! The old tyrant, I didn't know she was like that; aren't you miserable? But what do you mean – counting the widows?'

I was laughing with someone for the first time since my mother had left me. The directrice and her friend obviously could not follow our hurried, breathless speech. Already we were embarked on a conversation far beyond their feeble power of comprehension. But the directrice kept her eyes on me.

'The widows? Oh, there are thousands of women here all dressed in black with long veils down to their knees, so of course I thought they were widows. I counted fourteen passing in twenty minutes, till she caught me—'

'What did she say?'

'Oh, she said it wasn't proper. I began to wonder why there were any men left in the town.'

'Yes, yes, you're right. Why are there?'

'Because the women aren't widows! A week ago Mademoi-selle Portier went home because her grandfather was ill: he died, and she came back yesterday swathed in crape from head to heel, complete with veil.'

The directrice had caught the name; she inquired sharply:

'Mademoiselle Portier?'

'Mademoiselle Portier a perdu son grandpère.'

'Ah oui, pauvre Mademoiselle Portier.'

'Madame Maréchal's a widow. A real widow, I mean—'

'Yes, yes, I understand.'

'Monsieur Maréchal was run over.'

'Monsieur Maréchal?' queried the directrice, whose hands smoothed her dress restlessly.

'Monsieur Maréchal fût écrasé par une automobile,' explained the Englishman.

'Ah oui, pauvre Monsieur Maréchal.'

'Run over! How? There's only one car in Laroche and that belongs to Andrée's uncle. He keeps it shut up.'

'No, no, you're wrong; he lets it out on Sundays. But the accident happened on a Monday. I can't understand it myself.'

'He must have walked into it.'

'Yes, I expect that's what he did. Aren't we heartless? But I feel so happy I don't care what I say! I haven't spoken English for months—'

'When we're out for a walk and we meet a car, Mademoiselle Michelet screams a hoarse warning and we all scatter into the fields to let the monster pass.'

'Mademoiselle Michelet?' demanded the directrice.

'Mademoiselle Michelet a peur des automobiles.'

'Ah oui – justement; moi – non. Pauvre Mademoiselle Michelet.'

'Have you been in the forest, Miss Arabella?'

'Yes, we go there for walks sometimes.'

'Aren't you afraid of those dreadful boars?'

'No – I've never seen one. They're a myth.'

'Indeed they are not. If you stay till Christmas you'll see them hunted. I'll take you to a boar hunt.'

'Will you? I'd love it.'

'Won't it be fun! I say, I *am* glad we met. Aren't you?'

'Yes, this place is damn dull.'

'Well, I have an invitation for you.'

'For me?'

'For all of you.'

'The whole school?'

'No, no, don't be silly.'

He moved closer to the directrice who had sat down and

with half-averted face regarded him out of the corners of
her eyes. She had quite lost her pleasant expression. He
leant upon the back of her chair, and haltingly repeated
a message from Madame Maréchal requesting that the
directrice, her friend and the English girl would go to tea
with her on the morrow.

Smiling once more, the directrice accepted:

'Pour Mademoiselle Baschet, pour mees Arabelle et pour
moi.'

But after he had gone I observed her standing absorbed
in some gloomy reverie, pondering darkly, as I thought, on
some matter far removed from us.

How little, how very little I understood her!

*   *   *

The Maréchals were the aristocrats of Laroche.

At the time their fair name was damaged, but to the
directrice this meant nothing in the face of their wealth and
position as social leaders.

The next afternoon I met Mimi coming out of the salon
swinging her music case. She stopped:

'Bon jour, Mademoiselle. You are having tea with us this
afternoon, aren't you?'

'Yes, Mimi, I believe so.'

'Maman is in the salon. The directrice is asking for you.'

'Merci.'

I liked Mimi very much. Her kindly nature, her friendly
politeness and her cheerfulness made her appear almost
odd in that vinegary establishment. On entering, I saw
Madame Maréchal talking to the directrice. She was in
black, looking enchantingly slender and elegant among the
fussy furniture, the woollen cushions, the hideous hangings

and muddled ornaments that surrounded her, encroaching
upon the very arms of her chair, compelling her for lack of
space to tuck away her long graceful legs, and even to
restrict the movements of her head lest her long veil should
become entangled with a hairy plant in a pot at her elbow.

The directrice presented me. She regarded me silently,
almost shyly, before she said slowly and simply:

'Mimi has spoken of you.'

Ordinary words, but such French as in that school was
never heard, each word clear and distinct, the intonation
undulating and caressing.

After the sibilance of the directrice, I thought it magical.

I answered without difficulty. After another still more
thoughtful glance she observed:

'Already she speaks well.'

The directrice bowed; her ear-rings dangled forward. On
every hand carved mirrors reflected the action. They caught
Mademoiselle Baschet's kind smile. She promised:

'In another month she will speak like a French girl.'

I was dismissed to discard my school frock. My elation at
the prospect of my first French tea-party was quenched.

'In another month.'

A month! What did a month cost in fortitude that it
could so lightly spring to the lips and blow away with the
breath? Four weeks, twenty English lessons, eight walks,
with All Saints and the feast of St. Catherine, two very
small breaks in that same cripple month. A very fountain of
woe sprang high within my soul, and fell again in bitter
tears in the empty dormitory. . . . I dried my eyes, and
hastily dressing, stifled the grief which threatened to over-
whelm the afternoon.

With the three Frenchwomen I set out to pay my first
visit in the town. Several groups of women talking in door-
ways and shop entrances stopped their conversations to

stare after Madame Maréchal. She did not appear to notice, but the directrice and Mademoiselle Baschet glanced about them uneasily; the directrice bowed right and left continually. Her lips were set, otherwise she looked festive in a short fur coat. She walked very well.

The Englishman was discussed very freely. 'He longs to play the piano as well as Mimi,' observed Madame Maréchal.

'He never will,' declared Mademoiselle Baschet.

'Dieu merci,' said I, under my breath.

'Le voici!' they all exclaimed.

'Qu'il est grand!' murmured the directrice.

'It is a veritable giant in my poor little house,' laughed Madame, waving gaily to the Englishman.

He joined us, shook hands all round, and offered his arm to Madame. She declined it, making a slight gesture towards the directrice. The hill was steep: she took his arm and leant upon it. We walked up a narrow street cobbled and quiet, shadowed on one side by the castle wall, on the other by tall houses, soundless behind their faded shutters. The Maréchals lived at the very top of the hill: the front door opened straight on the road, and across the powder-blue paint was scrawled in huge white chalk letters:

Maison Hantée

Madame Maréchal smothered an exclamation that, bitten back as it was, nearly became a scream. She had turned very pale. The directrice stared at the ground. Mademoiselle Baschet furtively crossed herself, and the Englishman scrubbed at the wicked inscription with his handkerchief. Over his shoulder he said:

'By jove, this is beyond a joke.'

Madame recovered herself before the letters were obliterated.

'What a welcome for Miss Arabella the first time she comes! I trust she will not run away from "la maison hantée?"'

'Non, madame, au contraire.'

Directly the door had closed upon us the directrice and her friend burst into vociferous questions. The discussion that followed was too rapid and complicated for me to understand, though it was plain that they were horrified and indignant. To escape the incomprehensible hubbub the Englishman and I went into the garden.

Carved out of solid rock, it hung perilously over a precipice. The castle and the old church were level with us; the new church, brilliantly white in the sunshine, lay below us. I looked down at the narrow twisted streets, the crooked flights of steps leading from one miniature boulevard to another, the grim donjon and the town gates that Rose had told me were still locked every night.

Some nuns were walking with their orphans and their garments swept the fallen leaves aside in golden brown waves. A solemn curé, his cassock flapping, bowed to them. Everywhere the pigeons were flying.

'Still in the Middle Ages,' said the Englishman, leaning on the wall, 'Jeanne d'Arc rode through those gates.'

'I have heard that dozens of times.'

'So have I. Sorry.'

'Agnès Sorel is buried in the castle.'

'So I've heard. Look here, all that sort of thing sounds best in French. We're talking English and I've been looking forward to it, "Mees" Arabella.'

'Very well. Tell me about the writing on the door.'

'Street children.'

'Your reticence may be perfectly correct but it's not entertaining.'

I moved towards the house. He put his hands together.

'Don't go in. I really can't tell you any more because, you see, it's never mentioned.'

'Why do people think this house is haunted?'

'Oh, it's just nonsense. You remember Monsieur Maréchal was killed in an accident? Well, he wasn't very popular, and for some reason or another people say he comes back.'

'Do you believe it?'

'Why *no*, of course not. I don't think there are such things as ghosts. Do you?'

'Yes, I'm sure there are.'

'Why, have you ever seen one?'

'Yes, I have. But who saw Monsieur Maréchal?'

He laughed uneasily:

'Aren't you tenacious? We had a maid here; she *said* she saw him.'

'Where did she see him?'

'Oh Lord, I don't know. In the house somewhere.'

'You do know.'

'Well, yes, I do, only it isn't very pleasant to talk about. She had a child that she swore was his, and when she got out she spread this tale through the town.'

'How horrible for Madame Maréchal!'

'Yes, ghastly. And she's such a good sort too. Now tell me about *your* ghost.'

It was now my turn to regret we had touched on the supernatural. One night my father had come in raving that he had seen a spirit in the lane, and we had not believed him because he was drunk. But he was so ill that, having no telephone near us, I was obliged to walk to the doctor's house and, to the best of my sight, knowledge and belief, the figure that he had so wildly described joined me at the point he had seen it and walked by my side with a peculiarly undulating, terrifying gait for some hundred yards, when, springing away, it vanished. My horror so prompted me that I remember running the rest of the way, and for the only time in my life asking the Irishman to take me home. Not understanding the reason for this exacting request to an overworked, overdriven doctor, he looked at me suspiciously:

'I'm sorry, Arabella, but it's not possible.'

I went home in a taxi, but I remembered the refusal and the glance long after the ghost, from long acquaintance, had ceased to appal.

I could not tell this; I could not dwell upon this memory, so many, many miles from my adored Irish doctor. I made up a story which caused the Englishman's eyes to open very wide. He became very silent, so silent that we could hear the conversation in the salon behind us.

'Well, have you nothing to say, monsieur?'

'That was all lies, wasn't it?'

'Yes, mostly.'

'Why do you tell them?'

'Because I must. People aren't strong enough to bear the truth.'

'You mean you aren't strong enough to tell it,' he retorted sharply. 'Don't you speak the truth to anyone?'

'Yes, I speak the truth sometimes.'

I thought of the Irishman again, to whom I have never lied.

'Will you to me?'

'Heavens no! Why should I? Why should I, or anyone else, reveal what they wish to conceal merely *because they are asked?*'

'In that case you can keep silent.'

'How stupid you are! That gives it away at once!'

He suddenly laughed, and his rather severe expression softened:

'Oh dreadful sixteen-year-old! Will you reveal what you think of this place?'

'Do you mean the town? I think it's "moyen âge" – a place to look at but not to live in, I read somewhere.'

'That's true enough. But I meant this house?'

'Oh, I haven't seen much of it. It seems very full of furniture.'

'It's valuable. Monsieur Maréchal collected antiques. Get Mimi to show you her desk. It was Marie Antoinette's, and she does her homework on it.'

'It doesn't inspire her.'

We threw bits off the wall at the jackdaws. The sun had sunk. I felt the Englishman was a companion. He asked:

'So you don't like Laroche?'

'Like it – I don't know it. You can't think how I envy you your freedom to come and go, to see things unframed in a window, to walk about without someone behind you bawling, "Pas si vite, à gauche, tournez." At home I'm free as air. Laroche! It's all the Cours Saint-Louis.'

'And that's all the directrice, n'est-ce pas? What do you think of her?'

I was silent. He bent forward to look in my face.

'Condemned on your own theory. Your silence gives you away. Do put it into words.'

'Why should I?' I repeated.

'Do you good.'

'Very well. I think she's like Mademoiselle Baschet's cat.'

'What – cruel?'

'Not exactly. As you are so solicitous for my welfare, will you do something for me?'

'Yes, of course. What is it?'

'Buy me some candles, and as you pass the shrubbery on your way to your music lesson, bury them in the dead leaves under the juniper bush.'

'Fantastic woman! Yes, I'll do it, but may I ask why you want them?'

'I have nightmares sometimes and candles are banned.'

'Arabella – poor thing – are you happy here?'

'No.'

Frightened at the vigorous negative, disconcerted at the truth he had at last elicited, even as I had known he would be, without another word he turned towards the house, and waiting till he was a few paces in advance I followed. At tea he remarked:

'I hear you have a cat, Mademoiselle Baschet. Is it a nice beast?'

'Savage,' she replied.

'Next time you come you shall see it,' the directrice promised.

The Englishman's glance met mine. The directrice marked it.

The party broke up. The farewells were protracted and intense, and the Englishman contrived to whisper to me:

'If I ask permission for you to go for walks with me will you come?'

'Yes.'

'I shall ask tomorrow. Good-bye.'

'Good-bye.'

'Shameless—' began the directrice.

'Your conduct—' added her friend.

'Disgusts us,' concluded the directrice. 'In fact, we are far from pleased with you. I shall write to your mother if you continue to act in this manner. It is highly improper.'

I was aghast: my French left me, and it was an English defence and defiance that, stammering with fury, I poured forth in anger, misery and premature despair. At sixteen, modesty is of new growth and winces at a breath. Mine was outraged, and wild with pain, I rounded fiercely on the directrice who raised her own voice to combat. For a moment the quiet street echoed, then the directrice gave way.

Mademoiselle Baschet shrugged her shoulders:

'You are too severe with Arabelle, my dear. She is young.'

'Too severe,' shrieked the directrice, 'how, too severe? Did she not pass a whole afternoon in the garden alone with a young man? Hein, trop sévère? Ah, qu'elle ne se gêne pas!'

Her usual calmness had entirely deserted her; she stamped, shook her fists, bit her lips and turned scarlet. Mademoiselle Baschet grew excited also: they disputed violently.

'I tell you I could see her the whole time—'

'You could not, you had your back to the window—'

'Never did she leave my sight—'

'Tu mens,' screamed the directrice.

So they contended all the way to the school. I was dumb before the thought that tomorrow the Englishman would ask permission for me to go out with him, that it would be wrong.

*   *   *

The next morning my toast had been changed for bread.

The meal had hardly begun when the directrice addressed me as 'Arabelle.' I had become in her eyes a rebellious pupil, and she was determined that everybody else should see me in that light. Dupont put down her chocolate bowl and laughed; Michelet also, but Portier raised her pale brows and turned her intelligent gaze on the directrice who smiled down on her folded hands lying on the table before her. They were flashing with rings, and her diamond eardrops sparkled viciously.

Portier said in English:

'You are wrong. The girls will not respect her.'

'Ça ne fait rien. Ce n'est qu'une toute petite Anglaise.'

She called Rose:

'In future Arabelle will have bread in the mornings like the other girls.'

'Bien, mademoiselle.'

'Tell Eugénie.'

The directrice knew Rose's method of communication with the kitchen. Opening the lift door, she called down the shaft:

'Eugénie, are you there?'

The cook whined.

'Mademoiselle Arabelle prefers to have bread with her chocolate in the mornings.'

'Bien,' responded Eugénie.

Portier's eyelids fluttered. The directrice bit her lips. Springing to her feet she said the thanksgiving rapidly and passed out before us.

I skipped the dreary prayer, and when a steady droning proved that they were well under way I made my way to the shrubbery that I might intercept the Englishman whose request would be fatal to any prospect of happiness for me. How deadly it was I very soon found out; how stupid I had been was very soon revealed.

It was a quarter of an hour before he appeared with a parcel under his arm. He prepared to enter the shrubbery when some little sound that escaped me warned him. He spun round on his heel and a minute later I saw the directrice. She walked fast, her head up, a slight smile on her detestable face. They greeted each other; she took his arm and they moved away slowly, still well within my sight.

Blind that he could not see what was at last so plain to me, even at a distance and obscurely.

He chose that minute.

I did not hear him speak, but I knew that he had done so when I saw her drop his arm. I heard her answer:

'It is not possible. You do not understand.' No more.

They passed on up the steps out of my sight, she always a little in front, silent, with stooping shoulders.

In the afternoon I wrote to my mother and asked her to remove me.

Dupont wished to go into the town, and I went with her to post it. It was dark and the lamps were lighted, a cold rain fell. She went into a hat shop and stayed so long that I nearly fell asleep in a corner. Afterwards we went to the bookshop and I asked for Marcelle Tinayre's 'Life of Madame de Pompadour,' which my mother had recommended me to read. The woman looked at me curiously.

'No, we have not that.'

I turned away. Dupont leant over the counter; the two of them whispered together and smiled. I felt so annoyed that I ran down the steps into the street.

'Hullo,' said the Englishman, 'have you burst your bonds?'

We stayed together, talking. Suddenly he darted away into a grocer's shop. He came back with a long parcel which he pushed under my arm just as Legros came up. I introduced them, but her manner was rude and abrupt.

On the way home she said that she should certainly inform the directrice of my conduct. She cast prying glances at the parcel under my arm; finally she demanded to know what was in it. I told her to mind her own business, and at that her face quivered with rage. I longed to strike her; I believe she understood what was in my mind for she said nothing more.

The parcel contained half a dozen long votive candles, which had to be hidden under my bed.

After dinner the directrice sent for me. The air had turned very cold: during the half-hour's play before bed the girls huddled round the stove reading fairy tales till Michelet, clapping her hands for silence, began to read aloud. Rose brought me the directrice's message, and holding a lamp on high, lighted me up to her room.

She was sitting with her feet in the fender, wrapped in a pink flannel dressing-gown, screening her face from the flames with a book. In spite of the fire she was pale and so immovable that she might have been sitting there for hours, but when she heard me approach she whirled round discarding dignity like a threadbare garment that would no longer keep out draughts.

'Ah *vous*, venez par ici, j'ai quelquechose vous dire.'

The stress in her voice was appalling. There was an urgency in the demand that smothered resistance; as she commanded so it had to be – I felt she would dissolve into flame, burnt up in the fire of her own passions. She was tortured, grotesque, significant.

As I came to her side she grasped me by the wrist, drawing my arm to its full length and half raising herself by her hold, spat out with concentrated contempt—

'Petite coquette!'

I dread the smart words can inflict; physical violence infuriates me and rouses all the obstinacy of which I am capable.

'Laissez moi,' I menaced.

She dropped my arm at once, or rather flung it from her, falling back into her old position huddled up over the fire. In measured tones, but with inconceivable rapidity she poured forth a resumé of my morals with comparisons. I was silent; she waited for an answer, but provoking no more than an unquenchable glare of defiance and wrath, changed her attack. Her next remark was spoken with great deliberation.

'I have written to your mother.'

The letter was lying beside her on a table; she indicated it. I looked at her spidery handwriting in purple ink, for it made of my address an unfamiliar thing—

'Moi aussi, Mademoiselle.'

She threw her book on the floor.

'And posted it,' I added maliciously. Having nothing left to cast away she stuck out her expressive underlip, ran her fingers over the arms of her chair, shrugged her shoulders and began to talk to me as a schoolmistress. During the rest of our interview she controlled herself admirably.

'Do you not agree that you have been very foolish?' she asked almost wheedling.

'How?'

'In allowing a young man to ask you to go out alone with him.'

'Not at all, since I am never allowed to go out myself.'

'Surely two walks in the week are sufficient?'

'No, I don't think so.'

'Alors,' pursued the directrice, 'there is nothing you regret?'

I regretted nothing and said so.

'And the life of Madame de Pompadour that you tried to buy at Monsieur Dupuis's respectable bookshop this evening? What of that? Quel livre pour une jeune fille! Does that not show depraved taste? Madame Dupuis was disgusted. She has sent a note! Doubtless it is all over the town that an institutrice at the Cours Saint-Louis reads about Madame de Pompadour. Madame Dupuis thought—'

'I don't care what Madame Dupuis thought. And what about the portrait of Agnès Sorel over the front door?'

'Ça c'est autre chose,' answered the directrice, again raising her voice, 'that is old. I did not instal it, and I cannot have it removed. Ignorant girl that you are, it is insured for many thousand francs. Besides, I always say it is Sainte Thérèse.'

I did not try to control my laughter, bent as I was on outraging this harridan.

'Why are you amused, insulting jeune fille?'

'Oh, nothing, mademoiselle.'

'I *will* know.'

She sprang to her feet. I said nothing.

'It is immoral to read about Madame de Pompadour.'

'That is strange since my mother has told me to do so. It is a very good book.'

'Oh, mon dieu – good!' burst out the directrice.

'Certainly, mademoiselle; shall I bring you the letter?'

'Yes, yes. At once.'

I did so. Her eyes flickered over the page. She read the title.

'It is that,' she conceded.

Turning from me, she walked stiffly to the window, standing tall and angular against the dark curtains a fold of which she held lightly, and with a sigh let fall.

'Incomprehensible!'

With that last almost gentle comment she dismissed me. I went out.

*   *   *

From that evening it was winter. Sharp unrelaxing frost brought down the last leaves in the garden, killed the last flowers, crept up the windows at night like white fingers against the black darkness outside. Our breath hung in the air: it was terribly cold.

On All Saints Day we went to church before breaking up for four days. The directrice had arranged that we should attend a special musical service at the old church. We started early.

A crocodile of girls went winding through the streets headed by the directrice and her friend.

Mademoiselle Baschet was so fat that she obliged us to walk very slowly while she took her time to mount the steep hill. Every now and then she smiled at us, or waved her hand over her shoulder to encourage us, as if the pace were rather pressing than otherwise, but she really could not help it. The narrowness of the street caused the nuns and their orphans who would otherwise have overtaken us to walk behind; another school fell in and Mademoiselle Baschet strolled into church at the head of a large and mutinous procession. As was her wont, she immediately covered her face with her hands and went to sleep oblivious of the furious glances cast in her direction.

Ginette and other day-girls joined us at the door. She dipped her fingers in the holy water; they touched her hands with their gloved ones and each bowed the knee before the high altar. The directrice had made a prim little obeisance, the other extreme of Portier's prostration, that swept her solemn mourning across the pavement in sombre folds. In a whisper the directrice ordered me to do the same. I refused, and passed into the pew.

The vestments were gorgeous, the service stately: the priests intoned, the bell rang, incense rose in clouds; harps, flutes, and violins sang from the gallery, the mighty organ roared like the sea, the church became a dark cave swimming in sound, the congregation lifting their pale faces and their supplicating hands – the drowned.

When I would have thanked God for this tide of music, when in spirit I *could* have kneeled before the altar, a black curtain fell over my eyes and I fainted.

They carried me into the porch where I came round a few minutes later to find the directrice and her friend arguing angrily in whispers. The Englishman felt for my pulse.

I was lying on his overcoat, and he was on his knees beside me, so intent that he did not see me open my eyes.

'You aren't feeling in the right place,' I said.

He dropped my wrist.

'I say, you did frighten us!'

'Elle parle,' the directrice proclaimed triumphantly as though she had pulled a string to which I had instantly responded. She remained at a distance contemplating me, but Mademoiselle Baschet came and sat down near me. I asked who had brought me out.

The Englishman answered:

'I did, and I'm going to take you back to the Cours Saint-Louis. Lie still while I get a carriage.'

The directrice moved hurriedly:

'Comment?' she interposed.

'Je vais chercher un voiture,' he explained painstakingly.

'My friend, it is not necessary; she is much better.'

'How do you feel, Arabella?'

'All right. I'm not ill, only I had too much music all of a sudden.'

'Qu'est ce qu'elle dit?'

'Trop de musique,' he told them.

They stared anxiously. The directrice said in a low, un-troubled voice:

'Arabelle est devenue folle!'

Mademoiselle Baschet inquired:

'You do not feel ill, my child?'

I did not, but I was cold to my very heart and shivering.

In the end, Mademoiselle Baschet took me back. The directrice and the Englishman returned to the service.

I remembered with pleasure that I had not made the genuflexion.

Later the directrice showed me a letter from my mother which had just arrived. It apologized for my disobedience and condoled with her over the trouble I had given. My mother added that she would write to me.

That afternoon everybody went home and for four days I was shut up in the school alone.

'I forbid you to go out of the garden,' commanded the directrice.

She kept the post-bag under lock and key. For my entertainment there remained the piano, for my exercise the garden, for my company my thoughts.

*   *   *

I spent hours in the recreation room playing scales; my fingers became strong and supple in spite of the cold, and their action as they ran up and down the keyboard made me think of high-stepping horses. Power flowed into them. Secure as I thought from interruption, with no person in all those empty rooms to overhear me, I let my anger and my misery go free. I hit the notes, and clung to them, and sent chords rolling round the room. I beat the instrument and knew I was its master.

Rose said:

'I did not know that you could play like that, mademoiselle.'

She was not well. I found her, in the morning, trying to polish the beautiful wooden floor in the salle à manger. She said she was terribly sick, and, sitting down, she took her head in her hands.

I offered to do it. We tied the dusters to my feet, and I slid about till a glorious warmth pervaded me. Rose sat and laughed, turned green, ran from the room, came back, and laughed again. It took more than that to quench her gaiety. She had far too much to do, and I was glad of movement.

I took a broom and swept the dead leaves in the garden into heaps. They were stiff and crisp, for the frost held everything. Plants shrivelled, footsteps echoed and rang, great icicles hung from the clothes that Eugénie had hung out to dry in the deserted playground. She had to carry them away on a wheelbarrow, hard as boards, to the kitchen. They melted all over the red-brick floor.

Oh, it was cold in the house, and in the garden, bitterly, cruelly cold and lonely.

*   *   *

I sat in the kitchen with my feet stretched out towards the stove, a book or the household slate on my knee. I drew Rose crouching, her head bent over her embroidery, her dancing curls falling on her cheeks, and Eugénie in her white coif.

The picture pleased us so well that we would not rub it out: we hung the slate up.

As Eugénie went to and from the stove, stirring, basting and peeping into the oven, her voluminous black gown swept my neck and my hair. A faint warm draught followed her, fluttering the pages of 'Ces Dames aux Chapeaux Verts.' She told me of her children and, listening to her plaintive voice, or to Rose singing Parisian ditties, I lost my defiance.

The directrice and her friend had not gone away; they were in their rooms entertaining large parties of friends. A great deal of very good food was sent up to them. Rose picked at the dishes before she carried them off and Eugénie scolded her peevishly; she was afraid she might lose her place. Nevertheless, she gave me some to eat.

I found the kitchen homelike and peaceful, but the directrice put a stop to these quiet, pleasant hours. On the third day she came down with a basket of exercise books that were to be burned. She demanded:

'Arabelle, what are you doing here?'

I stood up, sullen and silent.

'You are hindering Rose and Eugénie.'

Her eye roved round; catching sight of the drawing on the slate, she asked if I had done it.

'Yes, mademoiselle.'

'Who has taught you to draw?'

'Nobody.'

After examining it thoroughly she announced that next term I should teach drawing. This, I thought, would not suit me at all. She had not kept the arrangement she made with my mother. I taught English regularly to the whole school, and to several private pupils besides, while she had done nothing more to perfect my French than to forbid me to read English books and command me to attend Monsieur Brun's lectures.

On the fourth day my mother's letter arrived. It was bitter and biting. She sided with the directrice.

Esther had written also. Her letter enraged me because I cared for her good opinion. How could I, she asked, behave so badly, like the girls at school who hid notes in the laurel bushes for the errand boys? Mademoiselle Dessier told mother she felt horrified at my behaviour to the Englishman.

I tore the letter up – my answer was short.

'If you write me any more letters like that they'll be burnt unread.'

Feeling myself universally condemned, I became utterly confused between shame and outraged innocence. Since everybody appeared to consider me culpable, with the simplicity of my age I thought I must be. Yet a little green corner of my conscience flourished untrampled.

The Irishman would not have judged so harshly, nor so cruelly condemned. As all egotists, I regarded my sins through the eyes of those I loved rather than through my own, and measured my guilt by their opinion of it. Of these, he came first and would think least of it. He was, indeed, of this world. Never shocked, he drew truth from me as nobody else could; to him I told my faults as studiously as I laboured to conceal them from others.

He has called himself my Father-Confessor: he was more. Against vice, brutality, stupidity, evil, I weighed this one man whose puissant image was the strongest influence in my life, and he more than balanced all.

*   *   *

Many of the girls cried bitterly when they returned.

Michelet came before the others. She asked me to go for a walk and I mumbled a sour monosyllabic acquiescence. Even Dupont was better company. We walked in complete silence for miles under a livid sky heavy with snow. Thousands of crows flew low over the bare fields; our footsteps rang out loud on the iron road. On the way back Michelet astonished me by climbing a wall round the garden of an empty château and stealing some apples. She shared them generously. In the town she entered a confectioners to buy a cake, exclaiming with a grimace:

'We might as well have a feast!' I saw, while I was waiting for her outside, the Englishman strolling along the street, and he caught sight of me. I recognized him by his height, in spite of my short sight and, bestowing on him a stiff bow that I felt to be in its way a masterpiece, I turned back to a wrapt contemplation of the window. After my sister's letter I blushed to look at him.

Michelet embarrassed me by giving me the cake.

'Myself I do not eat it,' she remarked serenely, heedless of expostulation.

This was the day on which for the first and last time I beheld Monsieur Marseille's car actually in motion. Michelet seized my arm, and pushed me against the wall. Valiantly she took the outside:

'Attention! L'automobile,' she breathed.

After tea I began to write an essay in French. It absorbed all my attention for a week. I showed it to Mademoiselle Baschet, who promised to take it away to her room and read it. She kept her word, and sent for me one evening. She told me that I wrote very well, that she was pleased with me.

'See what the Cours Saint-Louis has done for you!'

The Cours Saint-Louis had nothing to do with it; I owed it to my headmistress in England who had driven a sound knowledge of French grammar into my head at the expense of her temper. Monsieur le professeur de littérature certainly tried to teach me. He made me read aloud in class. Peremptorily he would stop me.

'Can you not yet make a French *n*?'

I could not. He tried patiently to help me. It was useless.

'You make no progress.'

I looked at the floor hopelessly.

He took compassion:

'But that will come. Courage.'

It never did.

I remember only one incident in the weeks between Toussaint and the Feast of Saint Catherine. I stole a walk. I went to the donjon and the castle: I inspected Agnès Sorel's tomb and all the torture chambers. I returned quite openly, and as the iron gate clanged I saw the directrice in the front porch staring as though she could not believe her eyes. She called me to her:

'You have been out?'

'Yes.'

She hesitated, opened her mouth, but said no more.

The senseless rigidity of her discipline did not relax. I

defied it. I was obsessed by terror for my failing sight. It seemed to me that my eyes weakened daily: I could not see the big wall maps across the room, incessant blinding headaches proved the bad lights were doing their work, and made mine almost insupportable. Afraid to read or write, I sat and brooded.

I longed for the wild freedom of my home, for the fields, and the woods, and the narrow lanes; for the mad rides by moonlight on the hills when a rabbit hole might mean a broken neck, and the villagers rushed to their windows to peer out at us through a tangle of muslin and geraniums, flying past like noisy phantoms, and infuriated farmers wrote letters to the papers about their young wheat; for Esther's companionship, she who rode like a centaur, fought like a boy and jeered at everything; for old ragged clothes, shared jokes, books, slipshod ways, and savage quarrels soon forgotten.

Nightmare haunted my sleep. I dreamed that I was running – running – over rough twisted grass; something pursued me but I daren't look back, and at last I thought I woke. I would scream, I would yell, I would wake everybody to see what they would do. I thought I did; I thought my splitting cry rang through the silence, I waited for the light and the babble. Stillness . . . unbroken breathing: I had not made a sound.

In the morning I awoke exhausted.

*   *   *

The Englishman brought a pile of books for me to read which the directrice duly confiscated after one black look.

He continued to come regularly for his music lessons, and to judge by the talk and laughter that I heard during his protracted visits, none of the guilt of that unlucky request was ascribed to him. It occurred to me to marvel how he had explained himself at my expense.

When I met him in the town I scowled at him, and if anything can be gathered from expressive features he was amazed. What a fool, said I, and a coward! His eyebrows shot up into his hair, his mouth opened, he made as though to speak to me, but twenty-five pairs of sharp French eyes struck terror to his soul, and silently he passed. He had skates in his hand and a muffler round his neck. Anybody would have known that he was English.

Twice Mimi brought me an invitation from her mother; each time permission to go was refused.

*   *   ＼   *

We had a half holiday on Saint Catherine's day. The directrice gave a party for the girls, and a few female outside guests. Everybody dressed up: Andrée wore her brother's clothes unreproved, Thérèse came as an acrobat in silver tights – it was a pity she was so fat – Ginette in black and dingy clothes made fun of les vieilles filles. Her lovely face lent great piquancy to the costume.

The directrice, distinguished, charming, and very amiable, wore all her diamonds. Her face was heavily powdered, her eyes sparkled. She went out. After a minute the door opened a little; in the crack I saw her standing outside holding somebody's arm and I knew it belonged to the Englishman. I was infuriated that this woman should have written about me as she had. With my foot I kicked the door, and shut it. Three girls acted a play: it dealt with the regeneration of a lazy servant through physical jerks, who in her exuberance broke all the crockery. As each plate crashed to the floor the laughter rose higher.

Sitting next to me was a strange girl about twenty years old. She had black hair tied with a piece of ribbon under her ear so that its length hung over her shoulder. She crossed her legs, clasping her knee, and cleared her throat rather often, but she did not laugh at all. She said, looking straight in front of her,

'I can't think how you stick this.'

She spoke English like a Canadian; she had no French accent.

The directrice re-entered. The girl jerked her thumb.

'That old hunks can't understand a word, so we can say what we like. Isn't she repulsive? How I do hate her!'

'So do I.'

'Talking already?' inquired the directrice.

Really, I could hardly bear to look at her. She drew herself up in her ceremonial attitude:

'Arabelle, I have pleasure in presenting an old inmate of the Cours Saint-Louis – Mademoiselle Lucienne d'Herut Voile.'

Lucienne took my hand in a hearty grip.

'What were you talking about?' pursued the directrice inquisitively.

'About you,' answered Lucienne in English.

The directrice understood:

'And what were you saying?'

'How beastly you are.'

This was beyond her; balked, she shrugged her shoulders, and left us. Lucienne turned to me.

'Yes, I was here for two years before we went to Canada, and hell I found it. That woman is a bully, a liar, and a grocer's daughter. Are you going home for Christmas?'

'No.'

'Then you must come to us: we're in Moras for the winter. You couldn't spend the holidays alone in this mouldy château while she and her precious friend return to the paternal grocery. How do you like the stout Baschet?'

'She seems less of a tyrant than the directrice.'

'She isn't a tyrant at all, but she's terrified of Dessier – funny, because she has all the money. This school belongs to her.'

She uncrossed her legs, tapped her feet.

'Come on and dance. I can't do the frog hops that Laroche practises, but if we double the beat we might manage to get along.'

I asked her to wait while I went to fetch some shoes with heels. Grinning, snapping her fingers at the directrice, she nodded. The Englishman was in the hall, his back turned to me. I tried to reach the stairs without letting him hear me.

'Arabella!'

'Well, what do you want?'

'To speak to you.'

'As it happens nothing could be more inconvenient.'

He tried to take my hands; I put them behind me. Stooping a little, he pleaded:

'Do tell me what is the matter. What have I done?'

'*Will* you leave me alone? The directrice is on the other side of that door, and if she hears us I shall be blamed.'

'Why?'

'You idiot,' I said bitterly, 'you blind, complacent, fatuous fool!'

'Arabella!'

'Now get out of my way.'

'At least explain your reason—'

'I will. I'll write it.'

'No, tell me. Meet me in the shrubbery tomorrow at eleven.'

'Very well.'

Overnight I made up my mind that no self-justification should drag from me the directrice's explosive secrets. By action I was prepared to commit myself, by words I would not.

Next morning I took 'Ces Dames aux Chapeaux Verts' to the shrubbery, and sat on the wall well hidden from the house and the road. Chosen for me by the directrice instead of the questionable 'Life of Madame de Pompadour', the dreary comedy had all the drawbacks of a book selected for its conformation to a standard: it was sterilized humour. Andrée and Thérèse laughed themselves into hysterics over it in the evenings. Renée had given me a 'Life of Sainte Thérèse'; I preferred its mawkish sentimentality. The pictures portrayed the young woman in a variety of devotional attitudes, or wrapt in mystic visions, her eyes rolled up, her hands clutching her flat breast. Their delicious absurdity filled me with glee.

I pulled this fount of impious delight from my pocket, and scanned it with never-fading interest. A bell rang.

The Englishman was punctual; since the wintry weather had begun, the directrice had suffered him to depart without her escort. Today, as usual, he left the house alone. He came into the shrubbery furtively with his head bent beneath the low branches.

We looked at each other rather shyly. I said abruptly:

'I wonder whether they have been watching you from the windows.'

'Good Lord, I hope not!'

He continued fixing his eyes on the ground and speaking very fast:

'I'm going to ask you some questions: are you going to answer me truthfully?'

'Have you any right to catechize me?'

'You were very rude and unkind to me yesterday. I have every right to know the reason. Why did you speak to me so cruelly last night?'

I did not know how to answer, and turned away my head.

'You hurt me terribly, Arabella.'

'You aren't alone in your suffering. You haven't been shut up and insulted, half starved of food, and quite of happiness . . .'

My anger had left me; I was afraid I should cry.

'Now go away,' I said. 'Hurt you? I'm glad of it.'

He did not: sitting on the wall he encircled me with his arm.

'Don't you ever justify yourself? Don't you know that Mademoiselle Dessier says you are a "coquette"? You're not that, are you?'

'Perhaps. Did she tell you that?'

He nodded, and snapped his fingers in the air: 'I don't care that for their tales. But why have you been so unkind to me lately?'

I told him: he was horrified . . . he said he should go to the directrice at once. And I believe he would have rushed straight out of the shrubbery.

'Don't be a fool . . . it's all over.'

I jumped off the wall, and began to kick my feet in a pile of dead leaves. I felt happy and careless.

'How old are you, Arabella?'

'Sixteen. And you?'

'Twenty. Have you ever loved a man?'

'Yes. Why do you ask me that? You are very curious.'

'Please can't you see it's not curiosity. It's a lot to me to understand you a little. Are you ever in earnest?'

'No; that is hardly ever.'

'I am.'

'It's a pity.'

'Are you a "coquette"?'

'You bet I am! My experience with men has been endless.

My ravishing beauty enslaves them, my charm drives them *mad*. Now get off the wall, and run from the wicked alluring Arabella.'

'Are you *ever* serious, you ridiculous person?'

'Moi, jamais de la vie. Vive la coquetterie!'

'Heavens, don't bellow like that. After all, I don't think you know the first thing about it.'

'No, not the first thing.'

He laughed gaily, loudly, and, recklessly.

'Those women—'

'She – did you hear?'

'Yes. Hide.'

He did better. He vaulted over the wall, though there was a six-foot drop on the other side. A hand on the stone, a rattle of pebbles, the impact of his hard shoes on the road, and the Englishman was gone.

* * *

I did not see him again. His father sent him to Switzerland, and when he came to take leave of his kind friends, I was giving an English lesson in the first classe. If he left any message for me it was not given. One day the directrice detained me after déjeuner. She put her hand on my shoulder and smiled at me. In all her rages I had never disliked her so much.

'I am very pleased with you, Arabella. You are doing well. After dinner you may bring your books and sit in my room.'

Her room had the advantage of being warm, but I felt that her company was odious. I sat as near Mademoiselle Baschet as I could, and helped her with her knitting. They kept me till ten, and when I went, the directrice asked uneasily:

'Have you had a pleasant evening?'

'Yes, thank you.'

In the morning I had a letter from my mother. She wrote:

> 'I was so anxious for news of you that as Esther was away for the night I opened your letter to her. It shocked and horrified me; why didn't you tell me these things? I have written to her.'

Four days before Christmas I went home, after a terrible scene with the directrice. At first, with savage autocracy, she refused to let me go.

'C'est vous . . . c'est vous,' she reiterated furiously. She thrust a letter at me. My mother had written to say that she thought it would be wiser for me to return for the holidays; she wished an oculist to examine my eyes, but there was no reason why I should not continue to teach at the Cours Saint-Louis until Easter, as had been arranged.

I almost fell with joyful surprise. But the directrice was beside herself.

'You will not go!'

Mademoiselle Baschet intervened, shaking and impotent. The directrice shook her off; she stamped on the letter, demanded an impossible indemnity, threatened to throw me in the road, and finally shrieking like a demented parrot, she mowed down everything movable within reach of her long arms; ink pots, ornaments and books crashed to the floor; I opened the door to make my escape, and a draught whirled the loose papers in a nimbus around the frenzied woman. Some caught fire.

'Allez donc, allez, allez!'

A surge of delight swept over me and I lifted my voice with all my heart:

'Je vais!'

My mother had sent me some money: I rushed into the town and bought things for her, for Esther. It seemed a different place. Now I could see its beauty. It was dark, and the shops decorated for Christmas were all lighted up. . . . There were rows of little wooden shoes in the confectioners, the narrow streets were crowded. It was snowing.

I felt as though I had been in a cage. Before we went to bed I said goodbye to the institutrices and the girls. Nobody was sorry; I had made no friends.

That night I slept again in the little room over the porch, so that I should not awaken anybody when I got up. Rose gave me something to eat before I went, and we hugged each other. I wonder whether she returned to Paris; she hated Laroche as much as I did.

In the dark I departed by the same train that had taken my mother, ten weeks before.

For years afterwards I hated the French. If I had been happy at the Cours Saint-Louis it might have dispelled my impression that the world was a grievous place. It is in me to pity Arabella: it is not weakness. Of a stranger I write, who may tomorrow be a stranger to the writer. Compassion for another surely cannot be condemned. I will pity Arabella.

*   *   *

My mother met me in Paris. She thought I looked well, and regretted having sent for me; before we crossed the Channel she had decided that I must return. No doubt the lights could be adjusted, and for the time being I must bow to the directrice's authority.

None of my family had ever suffered from their eyes; the business of finding an oculist was left to the doctor who recommended a very good man near Salus. It was all very nicely arranged, and when, in the beginning of January, I went to the Irishman, my return to France was imminent.

Despairingly I looked round the surgery as though the walls could shelter me from my impending fate.

He caught the glance, and leant across his untidy desk.

'What's the matter with ye? Don't ye want to go back?'

'No, no, oh no!'

'Then why didn't ye say so? Ye need not.'

'But they are sending me.'

'Faugh,' said the Wooden Doctor, 'the oculist will give ye a certificate if ye manage properly. And they won't instal electric light to get ye back!'

All the devils of terror and temper that plagued me fled howling from his laughter. As I went out it seemed to me as though the blue and red birds on the frightful wallpaper clapped their wings like joyful cherubs.

PART TWO

Part Two

My father was a most inconsequential reader. He had several odd volumes of dead magazines which he kept in a teak-wood bookcase behind a glass door, an obsolete Encyclopedia, a History of the Bible, Orlando Furioso, the works of Conan Doyle, and the Brontës' poems.

When I was seventeen I found in the *Idler* for March, 1897, an article on Aubrey Beardsley, illustrated with a few of his more notorious drawings. I was pierced by delight, my imagination leapt.

Those ordered fantasies, those formal visions, these fairy things cased in whalebone, queer figures in cold blood cast from white-hot fancy . . . this curbed riot, this dammed river, how it bore me away! The Elizabethan explorer who climbed a palm tree and from thence espied the Pacific Ocean was not more aghast at his discovery than I at mine.

I began to draw with Indian ink. The first drawing I made was Jezebel in a striped shawl, her breasts naked, her black hair gathered up above her gloomy forehead, two dogs licking their chops in her shadow.

My mother showed it to an artist. He said:

'Send her to an art school.'

I went to Chepsford. We drew skulls and vases, and a girl who wore all her clothes. A nude model was unprocurable.

I was twenty-one before I had my first commission to illustrate a collection of fables. I liked the work, except when I came up against my own ignorance which stood in my path, an almost impassable colossus.

*   *   *

69

My father was rather proud. He scrubbed a large wooden table, and helped me to carry it upstairs to my room: we put it under the window in a strong light. Every morning my mother told me to leave the housework.

At the end of six weeks the thirty drawings were finished. The day that I posted the last half-dozen my mother went to London and I was alone in the house.

I took the canary's cage from its hook, and hung it from the quince tree in the garden. The tree bowed over the grass, and I lay beneath it looking up at the jumping bird, who drank, and cracked his seeds, but could not sing. Perhaps he was really a sparrow and his wings were dyed. I saw the sky through the bars of his cage, and the sunshine through the leaves. They turned back in the heat; the hard, unripe fruit shone green and solid. I did not move for hours. I ceased to question myself what was the matter with me. I put my face to the earth and forgot pain; it passed me by, the fear left me.

I *had* suffered, I was afraid to admit how severely. I was afraid to confess even to my mother, to make it concrete. I had hidden it within my mind. And now suddenly, inexplicably, the oppression lifted. Twisting on the grass I could not recall the sensation which had frightened me into strict economy of movement. I leapt up, the bird fluttered, and I went to find groundsel for him, searching among the flowers. It was July: the blood-red poppies had shed their petals, the lilies were dashed and draggled, the delphiniums were losing their colour, and their skeletons showed through the blooms.

The garden was so deep in leaves that I took off all my clothes. After I had given the bird his salad I fed myself on raspberries and milk. Then I lay down under the tree again.

My mother returned very late. I was in bed, not asleep. She said that I looked better. She had been afraid that I was ill.

'Do you feel well?'

'Perfectly.'

In the night the pain came back. It was like a fox in a bag scratching and rending to get out. My spirits trailed in the dust. The claws penetrated my sleep; dragged me awake and I sat up in my bed. I knew that I was ill.

*   *   *

The Wooden Doctor said I had cystitis. For three weeks he would not allow me to get up. Esther was not at home, and my mother did all the work. She carried up all my meals, and fetched me books from Salus. I learned how to keep off the dreadful fox by lying very still on my back: as soon as I sat up, the creature worried me relentlessly. Sometimes I despaired, then the doctor visited me and I felt better. He knew everything about the fox; he called it cystitis! He had assurance, I had faith, the fox had hideous cunning and for a while withdrew. Try as he would, the doctor could do no more than cut its claws.

People whom I knew only by sight brought me flowers and books; they came upstairs and talked fluently. I smiled at them gratefully, but all the time I wanted them to go away and leave me to soothe the rampant fox, the cruel exacting fox that no kindness, no presents, no knowledge could placate. Confidence left the Irishman towards the end of those three weeks; he looked puzzled, changed my medicine, advised me to go away.

He saw some of my drawings. Glancing at me he said:

'What an imagination ye must have!'

In his eyes I read a thought: it was my nerves that were wrong. At last, one day he said it, and my mother echoed him. A flavour of dankness in her remarks made me think that they had been a long time submerged.

I insisted upon getting up. I would not abase my existence before the fox that had entered into my body.

One day after the doctor had gone my mother observed:

'He is beginning to look old.'

Sadness filled me at these words. To me he was unchanged, but she was right, and I felt that living and loving were slipping by.

August, September passed. The leaves began to fall, the trees to rock. I was sick in body and mind: I cowered, I could not fight the terrible beast that ravaged me. Then once again it withdrew.

Esther and I went to stay with an aunt.

*   *   *

One night we went to the cinema. I sat between my aunt and Esther who crossed her long legs and took her pleasure nonchalantly. She had scratched herself up from childhood, and in the process gained indifference.

We were laughing. Suddenly out of the darkness the fox sprang with flaming feet and famished jaws, rending, biting, tearing. I wished that I could faint and be delivered from this agony, but my strength increased with the torture. A man in front of me had rather long hair. I wanted to seize it in both hands and pull his head backwards: I felt I could have pulled it off. The lights went up and we stood up to go. I followed my aunt and my sister down the street hardly knowing how to put my feet forward. My aunt's house was old, standing back from the road. It had no electric light. On a round table in the hall two lamps that had been turned low were burning. As we opened the front door, mice rushed to their holes. The servants were in bed. I had said that I would make coffee. I took one lamp, they took the other, and walked away down the long passage to the drawing-room.

In the kitchen I leaned my arms on the table. The fire was nearly out; only a pale glow showed through the bars; it was enough to heat the coffee. Before going to the others I warmed milk and drank it: the fox hated milk, so did I. Gradually I was relieved, but I felt exhausted and helpless.

Next day I went home. The journey was terrible. The bus went as far as Salus, then, because to walk was out of the question, I took a taxi. The driver stared at me and wanted to know if I were ill. I asked him not to shake me. We drove to the doctor's house; he was out. His housekeeper showed me into the waiting-room. My face burned and I despaired. I saw myself in a mirror, my hair falling over my shoulders, my cheeks scarlet, my eyes wide and starting. I sat down, and, hearing his footsteps in the passage, stood up again. With his hands on the doorposts, his head slanting interrogatively, he demanded:

'What is the matter with ye?'

'I can't bear any more.'

'Is it the same trouble?'

'Yes, only much worse. I *cannot* bear it.'

He became very grave and pensive.

'I think it would be as well to X-ray ye.'

He began the preparations. I lost my desperation lying on the floor half naked. My wandering glance came to rest on his intent face while his deft hands did their work.

'What is it, what do you think it is?'

'I'll tell ye tomorrow.'

'Today – now,' I insisted.

The Wooden Doctor shook his head.

'No, ye might get fancying all kinds of horrible things.'

'I shall if you don't tell me'

He wavered. Then:

'No,' he repeated flatly.
'Can you cure it?'
'Yes, easily.'
'Will it take long?'
'About a fortnight.'
Next morning I asked:
'Do you know what it is?'
'No, I was wrong.'
'Do you think it's nerves?'
'No, I don't.'

He stretched me on a couch and stuck all kinds of instruments up me. They hurt very much, and I should have hated anybody else to do it.

When he had taken them out and I had dressed he told me that I must see a specialist. He would arrange it.

I pestered him with questions. His eyes lowered, his mouth depressed, he said:

'I cannot answer ye. As far as I can tell there is nothing wrong. Ye are an enigma.'

*   *   *

The Irishman sent me to a specialist in Clystow who had a nursing home. I had not expected to go so soon. There was literally not a penny in the house. My mother had spent all the housekeeping money. I was obliged to write to the Irishman and let him know that beyond my fare I had nothing. Would he ask the specialist to wait for his fee? There was no time for an answer: I had to take the bed while I could.

Clystow station . . . the smoky, vaulted roof, the belching engines, the line of taxis, then the town, the tangled tramlines, the traffic . . . the fox stirred – death to the fox, the hunt was up.

Everybody seemed to know St. Ann's Nursing Home. We drove up a hill and stopped before a brick villa with the name painted in black letters over the door. A servant who had most beautiful legs stood on the steps taking a tip from a wan woman with violets pinned to her breast. Another taxi throbbed for her. Some of the windows were already lighted up, and as I mounted the steps I saw through them white iron beds.

The maid took me to my room. She shut the door on an invalid in an invalid's cage. My complaint had become official.

After tea I had to go to bed. The nurse drew out the mac-intosh sheet:

'Perhaps you will not need it tonight.'

'I am staying only one night.'

'A test?'

'Yes.'

She smiled emptily and went out. It grew dark outside. I tried to read, but all the time I wondered if I were going to be hurt very badly, and whether I could be brave. If only they would come quickly.

An older nurse entered.

'Mr. Maitlands is just coming,' she said.

He had the matron with him. In her shiny blue alpaca gown, close-fitting yet flowing, her white cap tied under the chin, her narrow hands clasped in front of her, she made an effect at once severe and sensual of which every movement proved that she was conscious. Her rather swollen lips were compressed at the corners; she let the lids droop over her eyes. Her height was greater than the specialist's. His small head sat squarely, his decisive and abrupt manner was mitigated by a shrewd and kindly smile which showed a very fine row of teeth. Another pale, dark nurse with a thoughtful, remote expression stood behind them. Mr.

Maitlands asked me all the questions that the Wooden Doctor had put: over old and trodden ground he tried to trace the fox's track, now almost obliterated.

'This must be stopped,' he said, 'it can't go on.'

'I have been so bad-tempered—'

'That's not surprising. It must be stopped.'

Wrapped in a long shawl, I walked to the operating theatre, and stretched on the table, which I thought very like an ironing board, was subjected to another examination. As Mr. Maitlands peered and bent he murmured: 'Perfectly normal, perfectly normal.'

It was quite bearable unless the instruments actually touched the fox's stronghold. Then furiously it scratched and bit.

'It's over,' he announced. 'Tomorrow morning I shall bring another man to see you. Now let us see if you can find your way back to bed.'

Sore and tired, I trailed to my room. I slept all night like a log, and dreamed of the Irishman. In the morning the thoughtful, pale nurse brought me some bread and butter and tea. She pulled the bedclothes straight.

'You mustn't eat very much. You are going to have a whiff of gas.'

When she told me that I no longer wished to eat anything. Instead I tried to comb my hair, which stood out round my head like a thick tangled bush, and washed my face in cold water to take away the bright flush of apprehension. I was afraid: my mother choked over gas, and I thought I should do the same. I thought I should be sick, unable to go home, forced to spend another night in this horrible tidy room with its vast windows, great glass sheets revealing monstrous abortive architecture and people rushing up and down the road active and heedless; the ornamental green railings on the red-brick wall, the path, the

conventional laurel clumps through my retina printed
themselves on my mind so that wherever I turned my eyes
I remembered them. How I longed for something natural –
a hole in the sheet, a coloured voice, too high, or warm, a
flame in the empty grate. And the expense! What should I
do when they demanded the money, what should I say to
the specialist?

'Is there a letter for me?'

The nurse turned as she was going from the room and
shook her head. Feet stamped outside, and somebody called
her. She ran away. The maid came to take the breakfast things.

'You have eaten nothing,' she said, pausing for a moment.

'No, I don't want it. Why are there so many clergymen in
the road?'

'There's a theological college.'

She spoke shortly, and looked disagreeable.

At eleven o'clock two doctors and three nurses filed
through the door. They remained by the fireplace, talking.
Mr. Maitlands detached himself from the group. He shook
my hand.

'You are not to worry,' he said in a low voice, bending
forward.

I stammered,

'What do you mean?'

'This will cost you very little. I am not going to charge
you anything.'

I gazed at him aghast:

'How did you know—'

'Ah,' he said, laughing.

'Did my doctor write to you? Did he?'

'Yes, this morning.'

My gratitude to Mr. Maitlands I expressed incoherently
and without thinking. I leaned back against my pillow
burning with thoughts of the Wooden Doctor. The idea that

he was doing so much for me thrilled me with delight. What should I do without him; at any time, well or ill, what should I have done without him?

*   *   *

'This must be stopped.'

The other doctor had listened to the fox's record, and at the conclusion he repeated Mr. Maitlands' words.

They retired together towards the window.

The anaesthetist entered, dressed in white overalls, and the matron.

A nurse moved the pillow. The anaesthetist pushed it under my back.

'If you are going to be hanged you might as well be as comfortable as possible.'

He had a dreadfully lifeless voice. His appearance was terrifying: a giant in height and build, he was bald and bloodless. His large blue eyes were red-rimmed and glazed. His hands moved like fishes. He set down cylinders and tubes on a table beside the bed. He was hideous.

'Have you ever had gas before?'

'No.'

'Are you afraid?'

'No, I am not afraid.'

It was a lie. He seemed to know it and to gloat. Everything he said he drew out inordinately, prefacing it with a humming stutter.

'N-n-n. That's all right. If you are not afraid it's nothing. If you are I can imagine it must be *terrible*.'

The two doctors approached.

'Miss Warden, we are going to examine you again. It won't take very long, but we cannot do it while you are conscious.'

The matron took my hand. The thoughtful, dark nurse stood at the other side. She smiled at me. The anaesthetist spoke:

'Now then, this isn't going to be half as bad as you think. You just shut your eyes and go to sleep.'

He adjusted the mask.

'Just keep on breathing naturally.'

I heard the gas, and closed my eyes. No struggle, no choking, only steady breathing. I felt the matron's hand on mine, and wondered if I were ever going to lose consciousness. The voices about me grew squeezed and minute. . . . 'Is that water hot. . . . I thought it was.' My hands opened as though by themselves, as though my spirit would fly out of the open palms, my head roared. Everything was dark. Everybody had gone. Alone I swung in an immense black space . . .

They were talking again.

'La berceuse de la poupée.'

'Do you know me?'

I opened my eyes. The anaesthetist was peering at me. My consciousness had come out of the ether complete and perfect; there had been no dazed transition. I remembered not to laugh.

'Yes.'

'*Very* good. You just went to sleep.'

I felt very tired and very comfortable. I did not want to go home until I had rested. Mr. Maitlands and his colleague were still talking together. Before they went they told me they had discovered nothing. I could go home in the afternoon. They no longer said 'It must be stopped.'

Everybody had gone except the dark nurse. I sighed with relief.

'I am not going to be sick.'

'Of course not.'

Her gaze was deep, intent, understanding.

'Oh, I have been miles and miles.'

'You queer child.'

'Where music came from. You were all gone, but I was never lost for one moment.'

'I know.'

When I moved I discovered I was bleeding. I understood then what they had done. The nurse gave me a bandage, and I went to sleep.

In the afternoon a fog descended. Nevertheless, I determined to go home; at three o'clock I was dressed. The nurse, coming to see if I were comfortable, opened her eyes with astonishment.

'You are surely not going through this? Well . . . if you must . . . but perhaps someone is coming for you?'

'No one.'

'Do you feel fit to go alone? You have no pain?'

I had none. I felt desperately anxious to get away.

The secretary brought me the bill. I was about to tell her that it must be settled by cheque when the matron took it from her.

'This is to be sent to Dr. Flaherty.'

I had tea at the Nursing Home, and afterwards, as I was powdering my face and putting on my gloves, the matron appeared:

'Mr. Maitlands has discovered nothing wrong,' she said. 'He will write to your own doctor.'

'But can nothing be done? Shall I always be like this?'

'You may grow out of it in about five years.'

Shut up with the beast for the rest of my life. The image of the Wooden Doctor alone between me and despair, between me and the fox's mask.

The matron continued:

'Don't be too cast down. Strange things happen at twenty-one. Be patient.'

*   *   *

We were having lunch in the kitchen. My thoughts were turbulent and harassing, and hearing a knock on the front door, I went absently to answer it, holding the saucepan in which I had been about to boil the coffee. Seeing the doctor standing in the open door, I put it down on the rug.

'How are ye?'

Repeating to him what the matron had said to me, I searched his expression for confirmation.

He asked.

'Is that all?'

'Yes.'

'I shall write to Mr. Maitlands.'

'You don't think it's incurable?'

'No, I don't,' said the Irishman decidedly.

I tried to thank him. He did not stop me, but listened as though he felt pleased at the words, his mouth curving and his steady eyes on mine. I was obliged to explain that there was no money in the house; however, I was so accustomed to telling him everything that I did not find it in the least awkward.

He laughed.

'Don't worry about bills – I'm not. Get well.'

My mother began to abuse Esther in the kitchen, and the house resounded with her shrill, passionate voice. The Irishman put on his hat, very much to one side, and pushed his hands into his pockets. He had never much social grace, and now he mumbled goodbye and tumbled over his toes as he went out.

It is difficult to describe his manners, which were abrupt yet gentle, gauche yet commanding.

When he had gone I laughed to myself, but it was wry laughter.

The weeks went by, and no word or help arrived for me. Bitterness stirred again in my heart as the restless fox tore at his fleshy cage. I drew, and when I rose from my work, I was often in such anguish that I could hardly walk.

One night I looked from my window. What a stormy sky I saw, and the moon shining livid behind black clouds; the hills rose up to them and mingled indistinguishably.

There could be no comfort in humans. And my mind could find no god. I seized a pencil and wrote angrily.

'There's no doctor.'

'There's only me.'

'Am I to spend the rest of my life in the vapours? The gods forbid.'

In the morning I looked at what I had written with wonder. It was sunny.

All woes grow dim in the sun.

Meanwhile my mother fell ill with influenza. It was not serious, but she was a sad, dismal, crotchety invalid who whiled away the time by audibly considering who should make her coffin and carry it to a pauper's grave.

I had another attack, and our father had a roaring drinking bout. Esther and I could not restrain our shouts of derision. To quench the stream of abuse we pretended to have hysterics and yelled and laughed till our father sat down in his armchair. Crossing his legs, and holding a sodden cigarette stump, he ejaculated softly:

'You little bitches, you *bloody* little bitches.'

I banged on the piano with my fists. Esther's enormous eyes were wide and black, all her features were sharpened, strained. Our mother wept.

*   *   *

In the middle of November the Irishman told me Mr. Maitlands wished me to go into Clystow Royal Infirmary for observation. It would take three days. By this time I doubted that anything could be done for me, but I went.

It was a frosty afternoon when I entered that vast white building with a heart like lead and no hope at all. There were endless corridors, grated lifts, stone stairs; I tried to think of growing things . . . grass and trees; it was impossible. It was impossible to imagine that the foundations were on earth, and that above the roof was the sky. I saw flowers in people's hands, flowers swathed in green and blue paper; they did not look real, lovely as they were. They had never dripped with rain, opened in the sun, sucked life from the soil. No, finished, they had come into being probably in the deep basement, dressed in blue or green paper with curled petals, and clear, fast dyes.

I was going to Queen Mary ward. Outside it were an office and a kitchen. I was directed to walk straight in.

The staff nurse asked:

'Are you a visitor?'

'No, I'm a patient.'

I gave my name, and she showed me a bed, number thirteen in the right-hand top corner. It had a screen round it. The ward seemed to me an endless avenue of beds and curious eyes. Most of the women were sitting up dressed in flannel wrappers, but a few lay as flat and as still as the dead. There were a great many visitors, men and women talking and holding the patients' hands. Everything was very shiny. I was afraid I should slip on the glassy, polished floor. How glad I was to get behind the screen! When I had unpacked my things and put them in the locker I turned round and discovered that the woman in the opposite bed could see everything I did. She was staring hard and fixedly because, having no visitors, she had nothing else to do. I hoped I should not have to suffer under her inspection. Her face had the lustre of ivory against the pillow.

'You don't want to go to bed yet, do you?' asked the nurse, preparing to dart away down the ward. 'You could go out on the balcony, and somebody will bring you some tea.'

I wrestled with the door leading to the balcony.

'The other way,' said the ivory-faced woman quietly, 'turn it the other way, number thirteen.'

'Thank you.'

She smiled and nodded.

The sun had gone down. Directly I stepped out on the balcony I lost the feeling that I was imprisoned; that building was not so very much larger than many others in the city before my eyes, and beneath the flushed sky they all seemed small enough. Why, the Infirmary owed some of its elevation to the hill on which it stood.

All very well, all very fine, all very consoling. But whatever our lives and wherever they might lead us, however freely we have trodden, tossing our heads to the clouds, here, said the twentieth century, we must end, here the bogey will finally catch us, tip us into his black bag and away. This is the gate to the next existence. Who knows, while we are dying to the repulsive stink of methether, whether we are not being re-born in another admirable clinic to the reek of chloroform?

'No, you may imagine you're "free,"' I told myself mournfully, 'but sooner or later some institution will get hold of you.'

Beneath the balcony there was a square lawn, with a broad path outside it. A strange, magnificent tree, drooping and tasselled, filled up a corner of the garden. Thrushes and blackbirds, their feathers bunched up, hopped hither and thither.

I was beginning to grow cold, so after all, I went in for tea. The lights were switched on, the visitors had gone. All the lockers were covered with jam and paste pots. I ate my bread and butter rather discontentedly, wishing I knew somebody in the town who would bring me nice things to eat.

However, it was only for three days.

*   *   *

About half-past five they began to wash the patients. The bathroom was next to my bed and the nurses passed with basins and towels in and out of the open door. My bed-clothes stirred in the draught. A dark, swarthy pro., whose uniform had shrunk till the skirt revealed her legs almost to the knees, called out to me:

'Why don't you go down and sit by the fire? You'll freeze up here.'

The patient on the other side of the screen gasped and moaned. The woman opposite beckoned: she was finished. I went across to her. She also told me to go and sit by the fire.

'Come and tell me how they are, dear. We're so far away up here, aren't we? Number thirteen's a lucky bed. A girl went out this morning after a gangrenous appendix. What is the matter with you?'

'I've come to find out.'

'Oh dear,' she exclaimed, pulling her mouth down, and raising herself in the bed:

'Don't let them operate, whatever you do. One operation means half a dozen others. I've a sister-in-law that's never out of hospital.'

I looked at her closely and curiously, for it was the first time I had seen anyone after an operation, or, indeed, after a severe illness. Her breast was bound with broad bandages, the loose, pale blue wrap was pushed back. Her lips had no colour. She repeated without emphasis:

'Don't let them operate.'

I had a bath. Then on my flat bedroom shoes I skidded soundlessly to the fire. Three old women in coloured dressing-gowns were sitting round it wagging their heads and discussing symptoms.

'Hullo dear,' they said, making room for me. A small nurse, hardly taller than a child, wheeled another patient to the group.

She was a much younger woman who gave the impression that before her illness she had been plain and bouncing; suffering had endowed her with a peculiar and terrible attraction. Her large, intensely black eyes burnt in the wasted face, her brows, beneath a long heavy fringe, were drawn together. She constantly bit her lips, and with every breath her nostrils expanded and quivered. She wore a Chinese silk coat of cherry red, the loose sleeves of which slipped over her hands, exposing her bony shoulders. Slight, rather bent, she sat huddled up in her wheel-chair. The three women asked her how she felt since she had been up only once before.

'Better,' she said in a quick, rusty voice, 'I had some sleep last night. But God Almighty knows it's been terrible!'

They sympathized. In two minutes she began to laugh. Her white teeth were very pretty. She sat in the firelight like a handsome, half-tamed bird, willing to warm itself, but ready to bite any hand that might meddle with it. I could see that the other women were in awe of her. Suddenly she began to shiver and leant forward, her chin almost resting on her knees.

'Are you cold?'

'Yes, poke up the fire.'

I did so. Sparks flew out from the bars.

'What is the matter with you? Are you going to have an operation?' she asked me.

'No, I don't think so.'

'You bet you are, else what are you doing in a surgical ward?'

That was a new idea. One of the women said, nodding her head up and down:

'Never you mind. You'll be comfortable here. Everyone's so kind.'

Black eyes interrupted her with a kind of shrill vindictiveness:

'Kind, and what if they are? She won't care whether they're kind or cruel, or whether it's night or day. She'll just have to hold her breath and stop from groaning, or the sister will be round saying "Now then, you *are* being naughty, aren't you? Think of the others trying to get to sleep."'

She shook back the hair from her cheeks.

'It isn't everyone that is as ill as you,' rejoined the woman.

'I wish they all were, then they'd know! I wish my husband could feel a bit of what I've had to bear since my operation.'

'Now Mrs. Jones,' said the short nurse, passing.

The black-eyed woman regarded the little blue back with a reluctant and gloomy smile.

'That's my nurse. That's the best one in the ward. She's Welsh. You should hear her swear at the doctors! Look here,' she rolled back her sleeve, baring her arm. It was covered with little dots.

'Morphia. The nights I've had, lying on the wound.'

'What did you have?'

'Stone in the kidneys.'

She described her symptoms. They were mine. I said nothing. I was possessed by growing fear and horror. I felt a shuddering in my spine as though someone had swept it with a brush. The women seemed to gloat over me, to measure with their haggard eyes my capacity for suffering. They stared at me as though they would penetrate my flesh and discover what ill it concealed.

I made up my mind then that whatever the surgeon said I would not stay in the hospital. If I must have an operation I would have it at Salus, and I would ask the Irishman to perform it. At eight o'clock I said good night to the company round the fire. The black-eyed woman looked very exhausted. Behind a screen in the further end of the ward a girl was coming round. Her piercing screams echoed:

'My tummy, my tummy. Oh, mother . . . mother . . . mother.'

She sobbed and groaned.

The woman opposite, already asleep, straight and flat in her bed, opened her eyes.

'What a noise!'

Ah, what a noise! An uncontrolled body yelling anguish to the roof in a silence of subdued pain.

Music, thin and minute, ran like a thread behind me. Turning my head on the pillow I saw ear-phones hanging on the bed-railing. I sat up and put them on. At eleven I was still listening. I had forgotten the fox, and knives, and moans and surgeons, anaesthetics, morphia, terror and panoply of death. Harps, violins and horns wove a dance. The thick balcony pillar stood out against the deep, living midnight sky like the fragment of a temple. Fancy flew.

*   *   *

We were woken very early.

While the others were washed I could sleep, for I was not ill enough to require nursing. I used to have a bath night and morning. The water was boiling, and when I came out the patients pointed to me and said: 'You'll wash yourself away.'

Indeed, I began to grow very thin. This pleased me. I weighed myself, looked at my protruding bones, and said:

'How do you do? I haven't seen you since I was thirteen.'

I was obliged to leave the bathroom door open so that the nurses could fetch what they wanted; at first they were very apologetic and turned their eyes in other directions, but when they discovered that I did not mind in the least, they scrubbed my back for me.

During the night all the flowers were put in the bath-room in buckets so that I bathed in a perfect bower. Once I found the bath itself full of red and yellow chrysanthemums. I jumped in among them.

After breakfast the matron and the sister went round the ward. They stopped at each bed, and the matron said with her head on one side and a withered smile:

'How are you?'

The correct response was:

'Much better, thank you,' even if one were in torture.

The first time she put the question to me I said fretfully:

'I have made a mistake in my knitting.'

Her mouth opened. She paused in her motion – glide, hesitate, glide, hesitate – 'Have you. I hope it will soon come right;' and went on with her nervous satellite. The matron was very unpopular.

The Sister might have been attractive if she had not been so anaemic. The woman opposite pointed out a dark doctor to me.

'Him and Sister's in love,' she said.

The doctors came to see their patients with a following of students. Nobody came near me, nobody interfered with me in any way. I ate and read and slept and thought. My

nightgown grew disgracefully dirty. I wrote to Esther for a
clean one. She answered a day or two later.

> 'DEAR ARABELLA,
>> 'I tied up a shift in brown paper, but just as I was
>> going to post it we had a party and afterwards I lost
>> it.'

So I remained dirty.

The fox lay very low during the first three days. I felt
very well. Night and morning my temperature and respira-
tion were taken by the Welsh nurse. Grinning, she unhooked
the chart:

'You're a credit to us.'

*   *   *

The third day Mr. Maitlands came. He examined three
other patients before he came to me, and then he informed
me that an operation was my only chance of a cure. But he
would not operate unless he felt absolutely sure of his
ground; at present he did not. I must wait and undergo
another test.

I cried out like a child:

'But I must go home!'

I was utterly dismayed.

'You shall go home after the examination. You want to
get well, don't you?' he demanded sternly. I hardly heard
him.

'How long must I stay?'

'About another three or four days. Then I shall let your
doctor know the results. And I presume you will come
back here to have the operation.'

'I'd rather have it at home.'

'Well . . . if you do have one it will be a serious business. You would do better to have it here. Think it over. Good morning.'

He left me. After the doctor's visit that morning my screen was taken away because, for the moment, there was a shortage. Two patients were dying at the other end of the ward. They gurgled, and never came round from the anaesthetic. The convalescents' knitting-needles clicked tranquilly; pages were turned.

For the first time I saw the woman on my left side. I knew she was desperately ill.

She lay very high on pillows, fighting for every breath. The hollow of her throat was a black pit, the veins stood out in strained relief. Her head moved from side to side. Her nostrils, her dry mouth gaped for air. Her skin was yellow and drawn tightly over her beautiful features. Pushed back from her forehead her white hair curled behind her head. She called constantly for drink, but her voice was little more than a whisper. She was struggling bitterly for a foothold. In the day I heard her telling the nurse that she did want to get better, she didn't want to die. But at night, 'I can't bear it,' she said, 'Lord, take me, I can't bear it.'

'Try not to make such a noise, dear. Think of the others.'

'It's such terrible pain, nurse.'

'I know, but you mustn't be naughty.'

The night was made up of her anguish. Her husband and daughter were allowed to see her at any time. He sat holding her hand, his eyes never leaving her face. The girl leant forward: I have never seen terror and love wrought together to such a pitch of awful expression. After a little while they would tiptoe away, turning their heads to catch the smile she sent after them.

Something in her emaciated profile recalled my own mother to me with painful vividness. I thought of our own old devotion to each other, lying dead between us, killed by cruel words, senseless misunderstandings, wild and wicked recriminations. The likeness roused in me sharp regret, and pity which I could never have shown; my throat ached with grief and fear. I saw the future bearing down upon us, crushing my mother before my eyes, and I had been cruel to her; I saw myself looking into her dying face as that girl had for any sign of hope, and finding none. So it must be. That day must come unless I died first. It was all too late. Worst of all, I knew that, dying, we should not want each other. She had no human tie, and I, in the hour of danger, longed for my Wooden Doctor only.

*   *   *

When the nurse was making my bed I asked her if my neighbour might recover. She pursed up her lips.

'Possibly, for the time being. Not permanently. It's her heart that's the trouble. Nature will enlarge it to meet the strain, but in the end the enlargement will kill her. If she gets through the next few days she may last some time!'

After this, when the woman called for a drink I used to get it for her. I passionately desired her to live. She really seemed better, for she smiled more frequently and spoke to me. She had her hair combed by the Welsh nurse who supported her head in the cup of her hand.

'You are lovely,' I said and held my hand-mirror in front of her. The violet lips parted to reveal beautiful teeth.

'I was,' she whispered.

In the evening they brought back my screen. By the fire the black-eyed woman wanted to find out what was the matter with me.

'I don't know.'

'What have you come for?'

'To be tested.'

'What for?'

'Kidney trouble, I think.'

She burst into a dreadful fit of laughter. Her face was momentarily distorted, the black eyes flamed. Her arm shot out as though she were pointing and when she spoke her voice quivered.

'I've had it, now you're in for it . . . that beauty. You don't know what's in store for you!'

I stammered:

'Is it so bad?'

'Good God, it's torture. You'll be hanging round the surgeon's neck, and screaming the four walls down.'

She rocked with laughter.

'Now then, Mrs. Jones,' said a nurse.

I laughed too. I was terrified. The ordeal lay like a flame across my way, and I could not see beyond it; not for all that was dear to me would I let this woman see my horror.

'She's always laughing,' remarked a fat old lady with her leg in plaster of paris.

'She won't laugh long,' retorted Mrs. Jones.

She fell silent. Her eyes brooded on the memory of a shocking experience. Mine strained towards it.

Henceforth, whenever I was quiet or thoughtful, everybody said that I was afraid.

I hoped that Mrs. Jones exaggerated. That night I asked the sister if I could go home on the same day that they made the test. She replied that I should not want to.

'Is it very painful?'

'Pretty bad: it takes some people worse than others.'

'Will you give me a piece of notepaper?'

I wrote a letter to the Irishman. I could say anything to him. Then the long night began. A case was brought in early in the morning. A surgeon demanded loudly and insistently:

'Will you have an operation? It's your only chance.'
A weak voice answered:
'No, I won't.'
At six o'clock she died.

*   *   *

With the exception of my neighbour, nobody in my end of the ward had any visitors. We were all strangers in the town. It was very quiet and undisturbed up there under the great window. There were no flowers on our lockers; footsteps turned aside before they reached us.

At the other end people were running in and out all day long. There was the kitchen and the sister's room. The patients had always something to look at.

The girl who had screamed for her mother occupied the bed nearest the door. She was a young schoolmistress who had had her appendix removed, and in her own way she was remarkably good-looking. When she could sit up she spent a long time every morning and afternoon combing and tending her dark curling hair which fell over her shoulders to her waist. A magnificent bunch of grapes on a plate, and a tall glass vase with half a dozen scarlet carnations stood on her locker, her bed was littered with books and papers; her young man brought new ones each day. She seemed very happy in her convalescence, and had she not reason to be?

This girl and I grew friendly.

I was sitting on her bed. A woman student who walked up and down the ward almost every day, staring interestedly at the patients and swinging a notebook by a string, came up to us. She had a pencil behind her ear, wore her hair close cropped, and swung her hips as she moved like a person dancing a slow, sensual tango. Everybody noticed her. She began to talk to me:

'I say, you're a mystery, aren't you? Nobody can find out what's the matter with you. Wouldn't it be *lovely* if I could? You don't mind my taking a look at you, do you? How I should love to crow over them all! I really should be most awfully grateful if you'd let me examine you! You will?'

I lay down on my bed, stripped. Of course she found nothing; but she stayed discussing books and authors. I felt I had been years in the hospital; it was a relief to watch a healthy face without official headgear.

While she was with me the staff nurse brought me a letter from the Irishman.

'Excuse me,' I said, and forgot her. The doctor would not make any promise to operate before knowing what would have to be done.

Natural and laudable. I laid the letter down, bitterly disappointed. Not one word of comfort, not one spark of happiness to help me through tomorrow's trial. Other girls had red carnations. Why should I have this strong feeling for a man who never gave two thoughts to me? What was he – a divine image or a mute; a death's head in my mental revelry?

Seven o'clock. At Salus the doctor would be sitting in the surgery writing letters. On the desk, arranged by his house-keeper, he would have a few drooping chrysanthemums. The light over the front door would shine on the wet steps, the muddy, fallen leaves and the white gate.

The next day I underwent the test. The morning seemed as though it would never end. About three o'clock the swarthy pro. made me ready: we could not help laughing at the ridiculous sight of the red flannelette dressing-gown which had to be substituted for my Paisley shawl, and the long, white, woollen stockings. All the pins were removed from my hair; it hung wildly round my face. The Welsh nurse went with me; before we emerged she begged me earnestly to bear it if I could without murmuring because it was said in the hospital that Welsh people could not suffer pain without making a fuss. I gave her a handkerchief to stuff in my mouth, and as I did, remembered I had been told that when we were born my mother had crammed a corner of the pillow into hers rather than let my father hear her groans. I was wheeled down the ward lying flat on my back. All I could see was the tip of one woolly foot protruding so ludicrously that I laughed again.

'She's *still* laughing,' exclaimed Mrs. Jones aghast, and no exit with trumpets could have been prouder. After all, it was not so terrible. The handkerchief remained rolled up in the nurse's hand. Once or twice I had to clench the sides of the table, but my face reflected above my head in the enormous lamp was neither pale nor distorted. I was pleased to observe that, in fact, an infinite relief beamed from my eyes, since if it became no worse than this, the fox itself had often hurt me more.

The student of the day before was there dressed in white overalls like all the rest; she smiled at me on the sly and ran her fingers through her hair. Mr. Maitlands was now pouring water into my inside through a funnel. I watched him dispassionately. Then the fox, tracked to the very source of its being, twisted and turned within me.

'Can you bear any more?'

'Yes.'

'Still!'

'Yes.'

'Good.'

He let the water out. What a relief!

I became puffed up with my own resisting power. Mr. Maitlands asked:

'Did it hurt you badly?'

'Yes.'

'Well, there's no need for that. Stop me this time. Don't be in agony. Now, can you feel it?'

'Yes.'

'Already?' He muttered, and he looked at me astonished. 'Try a little more, now?'

'Oh Christ, let it out!'

'All right. That's enough.'

The life had gone out of me. They could do what they liked, I was too tired to be afraid. For a few moments they were busy, then I was covered up and taken down to the X-ray room. It was a special kind of test. The questions began again.

'Can you feel it?'

'Yes.'

'More?'

'Yes.'

'All right, that'll do.'

I felt sore and broken. I could not speak, I ached all over. A new sharp pain nagged at me. The nurse said:

'You were very brave.'

I didn't care.

'Will this pain go?'

'Yes, it will get better now.'

They lifted me into bed and put hot water-bottles to my feet and my sides.

'Hullo, number thirteen; how are you?'

'All right,' I said angrily, for I hated everybody. It was over, it was over, I could look ahead.

I was icy cold. They brought me some hot milk. I saw with some amazement the student standing by my bed. She had a bundle of papers under her arm that she had brought for me to read. Sitting beside me she uttered my thought:

'It is over.'

I pursued it further.

'Now I can go home.'

She raised my head on her arm to give me the milk, when I told her that I could not hold it, clumsily and tenderly. It was more comforting than any deftness. But I could not drink it. The pain did not diminish, it increased with every moment. I felt as though I were transfixed by a fiery sword; at each breath it twisted like a corkscrew. I heard the woman opposite shouting to me:

'Number thirteen, hey, number thirteen, you're not laughing now. You've forgotten to laugh, number thirteen. Hey, you, does it hurt?'

'Hush,' cried the student sharply. The woman muttered sullenly.

I rolled over on my stomach, buried my face in the pillow, sought ease if only for a moment, but found none. Sensation was so concentrated into one part of me that it ceased in every other; the ward spun round me, my body as the axle of that red wheel of pain, and to the axle like the deep heart in a whirlpool, there was an unutterable centre.

My mouth, my nose, my eyes buried in linen and feathers and my own moist hair, I yet seemed to see the clock. It had been four o'clock as I was wheeled up the ward. What was it now? How many hours had gone? I raised my head. Five o'clock. They had said it would get better; but it was getting worse, much worse every minute, and the woman opposite continually shouted to me. Stop her, somebody, stop her, and put me to sleep for pity's sake.

In front of my eyes as I lay prone on my stomach, my head turned sideways over my shoulder, was an expanse of bare, shining, yellow wall. Grotesque, fantastic shapes writhed, detached from it: monstrous serpents and trees whose plaited branches curved into growth and fall like fireworks. I saw the sea witch and the little mermaid; their hair was drawn upwards from their foreheads by a visible rippling current, their lamp eyes revolved; like a tangled thread the mermaid's coveted voice issued from her moving lips. Then they were gone, and only the naked wall remained with the electric light reflected in the glaze. My endurance broke. They might have seen, they might have come to me instead of forcing me to humiliate myself in calling for help. I was given aspirin. And then I was sick all night. Towards morning I slept. The patients being washed, breakfast, talk, rattling of crockery, the changing of the nurses, I heard nothing of it all. I woke as the matron paused in her inspection at the bottom of my bed.

'Well, are you better?'

'Yes, thank you.'

The sister glanced at me and nodded cheerfully. I wondered why I felt so happy, till it came upon me that I was going home today or tomorrow.

I stayed another night. A week had passed since my arrival; there was no longer anything strange about the long, shining ward with its twenty-four tidy beds, or the women's groaning and chattering, their courage and criticism on the very brink of death.

The four red hours after the test had taught me what an instrument of torture the human body can be. I felt that a seal had been set on my existence.

Mr. Maitlands showed me the X-ray photographs. One had a curious blur. Pointing to it, he remarked that he thought it was no more than a fault in the plate, but if there were anything organically diseased about me, that the spot was it. But he would not operate unless the repeated process showed the same mark five or six times. I made up my mind that, come what might, I would not go through that again if I could avoid it, nor did he appear to consider it necessary. No operation, no cure. So be it. Mr. Maitlands shook my hand. He was sorry. Nothing more could be done.

*   *   *

Directly I had dressed and cleared out my locker another patient arrived to take my place. She looked like a sad little black animal that had been taken to a lethal chamber. Death was in her shrunken, yellow face, and her whipped eyes. She walked very slowly with her hands clasped in front of her as though in pain. She asked me:

'Is number thirteen a lucky bed?'

I looked at her, and felt certain that this time it would not be.

'Very lucky.'

The curves of her mouth lifted as she moved towards it.

'Goodbye, number thirteen, I'll be out soon!' called the woman opposite.

Mrs. Jones' husband had arrived to take her away. Everybody seemed very surprised that I was going alone. My back still hurt me, and the sister gave me some pills in case I should feel ill on the way.

'I'm in grave doubt whether you ought to go,' she said.

'I must. There's another person in my bed, sister,' I said joyfully, 'Goodbye.'

Several of us went out together, and, reaching the street, went our own ways. Yet it seemed to me that, after all, we had only leave of absence. Sooner or later we should return to beds and knives and chloroform; the death these weapons opposed in truth afforded the only escape from them.

*   *   *

It was dark when I returned home. Both doors were locked. I seized the knocker in my hands and banged with all my force. Even that produced no more than a muffled thump as the door had been freshly painted and a careless workman had daubed the knocker also. I hoped the house was not empty; it seemed extremely likely, and no lights were visible.

Esther came, a lighted candle smoking and dripping grease in her hand. She pulled the bolts, explaining that she was alone in the house and was reading ghost stories. A fiery flush dyed her cheeks crimson; her features were heavy from heat. I held my back, it ached, and I felt famished. A teapot stood on the hearth in front of the fire, a table covered with odd dishes and lacking any arrangement was spread for some meal. A saucepan full of water with a plate of food on it instead of a lid simmered on the fire.

Esther and I sat opposite each other in the two armchairs. The spaniel, who was called Mr. Smith, suppressing his ecstasies, heaved a deep sigh, and extended himself between us. We exchanged a hopeless glance.

'Is father out?'

'Yes, hasn't been in all day.'

'Where's mother?'

'Upstairs on her sofa, glowering in the dark.'

Esther protruded her mouth and swung her long legs over the arm of her chair. She would make some fresh tea in a moment, meanwhile, would I have a cigarette? She threw the packet across to me.

'Have you had a row?'

'Of course. I wanted to move that damned saucepan. I can't bear it, Arabella. This is the only room we have to sit in, so I took it off. She put it on again, and spent half an hour on her knees clutching the handle and glaring at me over her shoulder. Oh, she's mad.'

'We're all mad,' I said.

Rousing herself from a gloomy silence, she turned up the lamp. We made some fresh tea.

My mother, in the long grey coat she wore for her retirements to her room during the cold weather, swept tragically into the room. Her face was set and angry. She sat down on a hard, wooden chair and began to cut bread for toast.

'Are you going to have an operation?'

'No, I don't think I am. They couldn't find anything wrong.'

'It just bears out what I have thought all the time,' she observed, 'that it's nothing but nerves.'

I felt injured at the coldness and carelessness of my family. I began to tell them about the hospital. My mother got up. She passionately threw her arms about me.

'My darling, I do love you. You know that, don't you?'

I did not believe her. Esther yawned and refilled the teapot. Our eyes met with deep understanding.

*   *   *

Mr. Maitlands sent his report to the Irishman. Nothing could be done.

'I shall always be like this. Always, always, always?'

He replied emphatically:

'I won't believe it. It's the nature of youth to recover. Be brave, Arabella, and fight it yourself.'

The winter passed.

The shepherds' lanterns bobbed in the fields all night. Ploughmen were busy. The bulbs in our garden pushed through the wet earth, and birds no longer swelled their feathers against the cold. Christmas was behind and Easter before.

I saw no more of the Irishman than a flying vision in a long, green car.

Ye Gods and Fates and Fools, no more than that!

*   *   *

On the Thursday before Good Friday a woman and two men were at dinner in their house at Henley-on-Thames. The shaded electric candles cast an orange light on the narcissi decorating the table. A fourth place was laid but unoccupied. The dining-room door had been left open, and occasionally a little boy's voice called from a room beyond.

'Arabella is late again, mummy. Do you think she is lost?'

'Yes, darling, probably.'

The little boy laughed merrily and pummelled the cushions.

The woman leaned her elbows on the table, cupping her chin in her hands. Her dark brown hair was brushed back from a forehead marked by fine arched brows. Her long green eyes were full of life and experience. She wore a black velvet dress that fitted to her figure; pearl ear-rings swung when she moved her head. Of the two men one was her husband, the other her secretary.

Both loved her; it was no more than natural that they should.

When, half an hour late, I arrived, she took me in her arms, and I smelled a delicious perfume arising from her pale smooth skin.

'Oh, what is it?' I cried, reminded of lights at night, and of a thousand gaieties that in the fields I had forgotten. My cheek against hers I felt her laughter quivering through her.

'Adieu Sagesse!' she answered.

She pushed me into a seat.

'Have you a pain, child?'

'No.'

'Liar!'

My feet were thrust into lambs-wool slippers.

The little boy who had been my pupil two years before rushed up to me in his little red dressing-gown.

'The same old Arabella,' he gasped.

He had grown though he was handsomer than ever with his darkness and his sparkling teeth.

'Let the woman breathe—'

'Arabella's better looking—'

'No, she isn't, she's as ugly as ever.'

'My legs are still crooked, Uncle Jack.'

'Poor old Bella. Never mind, skirts are longer.'

'We like her crooked legs and all—'

'Oh, I am so glad to see you all again!'

What a reunion! We had quite lost sight of one another since their return to England. I had heard of them in Italy, and back again in France. Then silence for eighteen months till the letter came asking me to take charge of Timothy for his Easter holidays.

What little I knew of the world I owed to his mother.

After Timmy had showed me his soldiers, and told me about the governess he had had when I left him (she called the 'aunt' 'a certain place,' and tied on my sou'-wester back to front, Arabella) and I had tucked him up for the night, I ran back to the drawing-room.

Major de Kuyper was sitting in a low armchair, reading, his excessively long legs stuck up at a sharp angle, a lamp on the table beside him illuminating his intent face. He seemed, as usual, more passive than active; his life had led him very far and now he was content to be still. The secretary, whom I called Uncle Jack, was bending over the radio-gramophone. Mrs. de Kuyper, flicking her cigarette in the fire, jeered at him. The windows were open to let out the smoke, and the curtains blew inwards. Mauve tulips in a jug were reflected in the great gilt mirror.

I curled myself down on the hearthrug with a magazine. Traffic rolled past the house which stood on a corner. My heart was so singing and burning, my thoughts so confused, that I did not know what to do with myself; I leaned back and shut my eyes.

Mrs. de Kuyper laid her hand on my hair. She rose, lifted her skirt above her knees, displaying her beautiful straight legs and arched insteps, and began to dance. Her feet tapped like castanets, the black folds of velvet whirled and swathed her hips. Her eyes half closed, she watched her effect on the two men with a smile parting her painted lips.

She hardly moved a foot, but her whole body was in motion . . .

Suddenly she stopped, her arms sank. She breathed a few notes, and went to the piano.

Her normal voice would have been far too big for that room; she kept it low. Mournfully she sang,

> 'Soon, too soon, the Spring will vanish
> And the year be fled.'

All trace of liveliness or mockery had left her face. When she had finished she leaned over her husband and kissed him.

The glowing fire had fallen to ashes before we went to bed. That in my room was no more than a handful of cinders in the grate. I undressed and bathed very slowly. Solitary footsteps echoed on the pavement below, and when I pulled the curtains aside I saw the angles of the roofs opposite sharpened by moonlight. It had been raining: the tarred road shone like ebony under the lamp at the corner.

The few men who were about walked fast, their heads bent, their shoulders huddled.

That morning I had seen the Irishman for the first time since Christmas. I was no longer a child; and I realized that I loved him with all the affection and passion that stored in my heart could find no other outlet. My hand trembled as I rang the bell. I waited for him with painfully thrilling nerves; it was several minutes before he entered.

We seldom shook hands. We did not now. He stood looking down at me and as his clear gaze rested on my face I felt my agitation subside into peace.

It was a little past surgery hours. I had rung up and he had said he would wait.

'Papa-doctor, I am going away.'

He nodded, his expression sealed.

'I have come to say goodbye because I may go on to Paris. I'm not ill. You realized that?'

'Yes, I realized that. Come into the surgery a minute.'

I followed him. He shut the door behind us, and stood with his arm bent against it, leaning his head down. His profile was thrown into relief by the brown woodwork. A shade of age, or unhappiness lying on his face went to my heart. All these years . . . all these years, since I was a child of twelve, and still he would not take me home. How much longer must I wander aimlessly, how much longer, or for all my life?

'How are ye, Arabella?'

He spoke with averted face.

'Better.'

'Not yet well?'

'No, far from it sometimes. When you hold the door like that you make me think you want to turn me out at once. You always hustle me off the premises as though I had the plague.'

The doctor straightened himself.

'No,' he denied, laughing, 'If ye had the plague I should be very interested in ye. Can't ye hear the patients next door shuffling their feet? They mean to be attended to.'

'Let them wait. They'll always be there. I may be gone for a long time—'

'No, no,' he interrupted. His tone was abrupt and melancholy and he moved restlessly, touching the flowers, lifting papers from the writing-table. Again he reiterated, 'No, no, ye won't,' as though protesting against a sentence.

I said to myself in desperation:

'Oh, why must I leave you again, you who are the only person on earth that I love? Soon there will be miles between us – one day it will be too late. Already your hair is thin and grey, and new lines have appeared in your face since I first knew you.'

My heart felt the need to share all its secrets with him. My lips held them locked. One day I would have to tell him what could no longer be borne alone: not for consummation, not in hope; for ease, in desperation. To lose my friend for a shadowy lover that could never be mine. Folly . . . folly. Tears rose to my eyes. I was ashamed and turned away from him to look out of the window. It was open at the bottom; the April air, laden with the smell of spring, breathed into the room; a bed of pink and red gladioli flamed in the sun. The doctor loved flowers.

I must go.

'Don't forget me, Papa.'

'No, I won't forget ye.'

He looked at me, quietly added in the same sad, strange tone:

'All will turn out well for ye in the end, I am sure.'

Were my ears so charged with hopeful fluting that they were dulled to flat despair, or did his heart really open a little way to me that sunny morning? I shall never know.

'Goodbye, Wooden Doctor.'

'Goodbye, Arabella.'

I stretched out my arm and drew a cross above his heart. He neither started nor recoiled.

'Arabella, her mark.'

He walked with me to the door. I turned on the step to look once more up at him, and it seemed to me that wherever I went the memory of his face as it looked then would go with me. Should I write to him?

Yes, he would like some of my funny drawings.

And would he answer? In asking this I felt no shame as a woman demanding a favour from a man. The thirty years' difference in our ages lent him a superiority in wisdom which I never questioned. The strength that withheld itself was the strength that supported me.

Yes, he would answer.

I ran down the steps, leapt into the taxi. The driver straightened himself and folded up his paper. The doctor shut his door.

My mind went over all this as I lay in my bed. Everything since had struck me like a dream. I had put out the light, and the room behind its drawn curtains was quite dark. The April night was cold. Little by little I drowsed till I thought that once more I stood on the steps facing the closed door, and, ringing the bell with all my strength, cried out:

'Let me in, Papa, this is my home.'

Oh, what a fool!

Adieu, adieu, adieu . . . sagesse.

*   *   *

As I pause for a moment looking back on these things I have a terrible feeling that it is impossible to live any longer; the light is behind me. Dear Papa-doctor, it is incredible to

me that you should be in this same world with me and care
nothing for my pain!

I will *not* try to forget him: I summon up my recollections.

April passed: never since have I experienced so pure a
bliss, so vivid a surety that it was sweet to exist. Bitterness
and doubting no longer coloured my thoughts: all that was
dark and troubled in my love for the Irishman subsided; it
flowed swiftly like a bright clear river from the early hours
of Easter morning when his face broke through my dreams.
The sense of his presence was so strong that he seemed to
be with me, breathing the air I breathed. Tension had held
me even while I slept, now it relaxed. I got up and dressed.
Church bells were ringing; a single shaft of sunlight fell on
a jar of daffodils standing on the table beside my bed, and
broke up among the yellow papery petals. Happy virgin
Easter, happy morning when the very idea of misery seemed
futile, absurd and remote.

Timothy and I ran beside the river, our hair blown back
from our faces. The breeze blew against the current, wrin-
kling the smooth surface into ripples against the swans'
breasts as they chased one another for the bread we threw
to them.

Thousands of celandines like varnished stars spattered
the grass. A man with his baby in a boat held the child with
one hand while he paddled with the other; a girl in a bright
scarlet jersey polished the metal-work of her motor-boat.
Everything that I saw is sharpened by memory into fade-
less pictures.

No doubt I was in pain sometimes, or tired, or cold, or
cross, but I cannot remember it. I lived in a contained ecstasy.
The current's smoothness might well deceive me as to its
velocity; I was travelling faster than I knew.

*   *   *

Then the cut was dealt to me that divided my life into two parts. The period I approach was one of intense misery to me: I cannot write about it now without trembling; yet I am urged to do it. It is very difficult and must be done with the utmost simplicity or I shall turn aside to darkness where lucidity is hopelessly lost in the incoherent exploration of sensations.

So might a man released by death from torture watch his own body burning. Through suffering or triumph there comes a time to all of us when one figure dominates our universe, and that our own. We are egotists because we are obliged to be: a charmed circle has been drawn around us. From the centre we see people and circumstances withdrawn at a distance into the shadows. There is no counting or reckoning. There is no communication.

We are alone.

PART THREE

Part Three

I did not go to Paris. Instead I went to live with my cousin in Oxfordshire. Within a week I received a letter from the Wooden Doctor in answer to one of mine. The secret of my love had revealed itself to him at last; it had come to such uncontrollable strength that I was too frail and narrow a vessel to hold it longer in captivity. It is a proof of my chaotic state that I cannot recall in the least how he found out.

He wrote:

> 'MY DEAR CHILD,
>
> 'What can be the matter with you?
>
> 'This affliction is even more difficult to deal with than your other. It is an everyday occurrence for me to say "I am afraid I must hurt you but you will be better after . . ." And so . . .
>
> 'If you were a little older I should perhaps tell you a true story, but if you were a little older you would not want to hear it, although it might explain why I can be no more to you than a Father Confessor.'

I read this letter several times. My hands were trembling and I felt a sensation like cold fingers creeping up my temples. I was standing in the stone porch; beyond the deep shadow cast by its projection the sun was shining in the garden. I walked down the path and leaned upon the wall, pressing the hard stone into my breast. Here I read the letter again.

'If you were a little older.'

If that had been, would he have loved me?

I remembered asking him, after some escapade, what he thought of me. He had regarded me smiling but silent, and I had read his answer in his eyes. He thought me a child . . . and as a child he had treated me, my Papa-doctor, a tender and indulgent father.

I wanted to go to him. It was the only clear thought in my head.

My cousin, in a blue linen overall which she wore to milk the cows, ran out of the door, her face radiant with morning freshness. She held the gong and beat it. As I approached her, her expression changed. The brass gong swung still, faintly humming, catching the sunlight in blinding flashes.

'What is the matter?'

'I must go home. I'll come back tomorrow.'

'Is anybody ill?'

'No. I am going to see a man.'

There were other questions and answers but I have forgotten them.

In the middle of the day her husband drove me to Coln-ford to catch the bus. He regarded me inquisitively. My clothes were carelessly put on and I had overlooked my gloves.

At four o'clock I was in Salus. The doctor would be on his rounds. It was market-day and hot; there were crowds in the streets. It was all so familiar, and the feeling I had was so very strange. People smiled at me and spoke to me. With an idea of escaping, I made my way to our old school. The iron gate creaked as it had done when I was sixteen and safe behind it, the dusty laurels looked as forlorn as when a junior I had been despatched by older girls with wondering curiosity, to search among the dead dry leaves underneath them for notes left by the errand boys they ogled from the windows in murky courtship. There were the flower beds bordered with rough white stones round which we had played tag, and the ragged fir-tree whose shade was so grateful to us when the scraggy lawn was burnt brown by the sun. I pulled the old brass bell; while I waited, half a dozen girls came out of the back door in blazers, bouncing a net-ball. I recognized in these long-legged adolescents children who had been with Esther in the lower forms when I was at school. Their faces had grown sharper and thinner. They did not know me. Away they ran towards the playing field, giggling, shouting and throwing the ball. The door was opened by the house-keeper, a widow, who had beautiful, fiery red hair and a careworn expression; we were old friends, and she asked me in to tea. As we went along the passage between the rows of pegs, I looked for one in a dark corner that had been mine; I found it, my name still inscribed underneath on a ditty card fixed to the wall by drawing pins. I had chosen it for its obscurity because otherwise it would have been discovered that I never had a hat. I could not take a step without my younger self rising before me.

Tea was set in the dining-room. That window, draped in white net curtains, was the one from which I had waved to the Irishman driving along the road. I remembered his side-long and gay smile; his hair was greying then; mine down my back in two plaits . . .

Mrs. Lewis, pouring tea for three silent boarders, asked after my mother who used to take her flowers from our garden. I replied that I had not been home.

'I have only come over for one night.'

'You are very pale,' she observed abruptly, gazing at me for a moment intently, 'Are you tired?'

'A little!'

'I remember now; you were ill in the autumn, your mother told me. Are you quite cured?'

'Not yet. I am better. Mrs. Lewis, I should like to wait in the school till seven o'clock if I may.'

'Of course. But you know that there is a bus to King's Capel on market-days at half-past six? You don't look fit to walk out there.'

'I am going to see the doctor at seven.'

After the tea was over I went upstairs to the classrooms. The same old woman, smelling of snuff, was working with a broom and pail looking just as she had in my time, her hair scraped tightly in greasy wisps over her egg-shaped skull, showing the parchment-coloured scalp, her filthy withered neck disappearing into a blue cotton gown, her eyes like glue. She used to fly into furious passions with me, and chase me up and down the stairs, for she was very active and ill-humoured. I said:

'Hullo, Mary.'

She stared at me solemnly. Suddenly a smile showed her gums:

'It's Miss Arabella?'

'Yes. Do you remember me?'

'Ah, I do. You're just the same. But I haven't seen you for a long time, dearie. Are you married?'

'No, Mary. Do you still like snuff?'

She nodded. I gave her sixpence which she put in the pocket of her sacking apron. Leaning on her broom, she continued to regard me, chuckling.

'Do you remember when Esther put a dead snake in Mavis Hill's desk?'

'Ah, I do. And when I shut you in the cellar along with Miss Annie, and you stuck your arms through the grating into the road. Oh Lord, Lord, it's a long time ago.'

Little by little the animation left her face. Her mouth hanging half open, and snuffling through her nose, she picked up the bucket and shuffled off. I was glad; I never liked her. I had never really liked the school, or this panelled classroom, and had I felt like questioning myself, might have asked what I was doing there rather than any-where else. But I did not, for nothing mattered until seven o'clock.

I continued to wander around the room where nothing was changed: the same sham-alabaster clock with gilt hands, the same litter of coloured chalks on the mantelpiece, the same dusty blackboards, the same dingy collection of books in the cupboard covered in brown paper, the same cracked bell on the table. I found also my own desk; at thirteen I had grown so much too tall for it that I had begun to stoop in consequence of sitting at it, and my headmistress, an indulgent woman, had the legs lengthened with wooden blocks so that it stood out among the rest. It had been repainted, but the great circle that I had traced with a compass biting deep into the lid remained clearly to be seen. Everyone had been very angry with me, and I was punished severely.

I heard my headmistress now. 'Why do you *do* these foolish things?' Ah, what a quantity of stupidities, equally sense-less and enduring, had I not committed since then!

I took a volume from the shelves and sat with it open before me on the desk. I read two lines over and over again without thinking about them at all till they were graven as deep on my mind as the circle was on the wood.

'Whither, oh lonely ship, thy white sails crowding,
Leaning upon the bosom of the urgent West . . .'

When the alabaster clock pointed to quarter to seven I pre-pared to go, scrutinizing myself in the small mirror hanging outside the door. My face was very white and rather grimy; I cleaned it and pushed back my hair. Mrs. Lewis had gone out. I left the house, and walked swiftly to the doctor's.

It was a mild, sweet evening; the flowering trees in the gardens were budding, there was a fragrance of apple blossom in the air. The doctor had not yet returned. I stood in the waiting-room leaning my arms on the window-sill, my heart beating in great slow thumps, cold with fear and unhappiness. The surgery door opened; in the kitchen the servants talked, footsteps passed to and fro. In another room a clock chimed the quarter.

I was aware that the doctor stood in the doorway looking at me, but I could not turn my head; I felt as though I were strangling. At last I moved and encountered his grave, still sorrowful glance.

'Come into the surgery, I want to speak to ye. Sit down.'

He himself sat at his desk; I stared out of the window. Above the frosted glass that hid the garden brilliant green chestnut leaves were visible against the vivid blue sky: I kept my gaze on them, and as long as I shall exist that branch will live in my memory.

'Admit that I have courage.'

'I do admit it. Ye look like death.'

It was death. He did not love me. He never would love me. What ghost walked beside him he would not tell; she would be there always. Through all eternity we should never touch.

'My dear, it's impossible; autumn cannot mate with spring—'

'Poor spring has farther to go.'

'That's true. Ye don't realize – I am old enough to be your father.'

He leaned over the desk. 'Arabella, Arabella, think! How could it be? I am over fifty, you are twenty odd; such marriages aren't happy. They may be for a year or two – no longer. Ye don't realize,' he repeated.

'I realize many things . . . too many. You don't love me

and now you will never learn. If you did, age would make no difference.'

'We cannot change ourselves one way or another. Child, it's all wrong.'

'No, no.'

'Yes, it is. Did ye think that I thought of ye . . . like ye have thought of me?'

I shook my head.

'Have ye had any reason to suppose that I did?'

'No . . . no . . . never. It's all my fault. You have been perfect. Were you very horrified?'

'Not horrified,' said the doctor sighing, 'I was surprised.'

'You ought to be proud: I should have been.'

He looked astonished at my fiery change of tone.

'In a way I was.'

'Do you want me to forget?'

The doctor rose and stood at the window: someone in the garden was digging. We could hear the spade entering the earth, and thumping it down. With his face averted, he said in a low voice:

'For your sake – I do. Oh, child, don't look so despairing! There is no other way, and ye are young, ye are young, ye will forget. In six months ye will have forgotten, will call yourself a fool.'

'Will that be comfort?'

'It will be cure! I know, believe me, Arabella.'

I could not. For the first time in my life I saw limits to his comprehension: even as he proved the perfection of his manhood he discovered a lack of vision. He could not lay a hand upon the wound, because he denied that it existed. I saw trouble on his brow, yet I thought he regarded me quizzically, and the strange reflection took possession of me that there were some things he could not see as clearly as I, some that he missed altogether.

'How long have you known me?'

'Since ye were so high,' he replied with a relieved expression, measuring the stature of a child of twelve. I lifted my eyes and looked him full in the face.

'Since then I have loved you. There never has been any other man. One thing I can do, I can love. I am going.'

'In six months—'

'I hope I don't cry in the street.'

'No, ye won't cry. Hold your head up. I am sorry the doctor was too old.'

He opened the door. I stood on the step, the street was empty, the birds in his front garden were singing. Everything seemed so peaceful, and so empty. The account was paid for all my sins – past and to come. The doctor spoke a few words of comfort with a terrible finality. I took a step away from him, whirled round panting:

'Kiss me, Papa.'

He stooped, laid his lips on mine for the only time in our lives. Then I ran blindly along the road, tears pouring down my face.

Of that interview I have never told a soul. I believe he imagined that one day a happy woman might come to thank him for his skilful treatment of an infatuated schoolgirl. He did not understand in the very least.

Thus was the Wooden Doctor.

*   *   *

My tears soon ceased. Of what use to cry? I walked home by the river, loitering in the meadows. The water for all its swiftness looked calm as a sheet of glass; no ripple or breath of air disturbed the willows' reflections.

I found the doors open; nobody, however, appeared to be

in the house. My mother was weeding in the garden, throwing the rubbish that she pulled out of the ground into a white enamel bucket with a hole in the side and a rusty handle that she had used for this purpose as long as I could remember. The red chestnut would soon flower. The deep crimson tulips were going over. She was amazed to see me. She began to question me: why had I come, had anything happened, how long did I think of staying?

I lied . . . and the thought stabbed me through and through that there would be no one now to whom I could tell the truth.

Had my mother known what had really brought me to Salus there is no doubt that she would have been deeply shocked. Esther was away. We ate our supper together in the kitchen, and when we had washed the dishes by the light of a fairy lamp we went into the drawing-room to shut up the windows so that the damp air should not relax the piano strings. My mother stretched her fingers over the keys; she lifted her hands that housework had reduced to bones and sinews with black chaps and broken nails, and brought them down on the opening chords of the Pathetic Sonata. How well she played, though her wrists were stiff. It was unbearable: the majesty, the poignancy pierced the soul.

'Good night, mother, I am going to bed.'

'Good night. I shall wait up for your father,' she answered while she continued softly to play. After I shut the door I could no longer hear the music, but I did not sleep until dawn. The lights of Salus strung against the hills like jewels were extinguished, the owls shrieked. A night bird jarred up and down the scale a wild and hideous fantasia. The leaves of the holly tree rattled drily.

*   *   *

I returned to my cousin's. The Irishman wrote to me and gave me two promises: If he decided to marry he would tell me before the news could creep round to my ears through any other channel; if I were very ill he would come to me. In conclusion, he wrote:

> 'I feel so sorry for you, Arabella. I should like to comfort you, and, believe me, I *do* understand, more than you think, but what will you?
>
> 'We cannot change one way or another; things are as they are.
>
> 'I shall always have a very kind thought for a very brave child.'

I read it, and put it away with his other letters.

My cousin had a beautiful face. Those delicate features, those laughing, shining eyes, that cunning mouth, all that fascination so frequently before me, so contentedly blooming beside the husband she adored, tortured me. Savagely I envied her, not for what she had, but for what she might have had. To myself I cried: 'J'ai perdu, perdu, perdu; elle auriait gagnée!'

Full bitterness was mine, but my habit of deception hid it all. Outwardly I led a commonplace and happy existence: inwardly I seethed with jealousy and shame, and an aching loss.

I could not attract the man I loved: henceforth I should walk in utter humiliation. Twenty lovers would not atone for it. I look at those words now that I have written them down, admitting their truth. Arabella, from the heights of folly and the depths of despair I trounce you, denounce you, curse you, flout you for a fool.

I wish I could inspire one half the devotion I have given!

*   *   *

I had lost my friend because I loved him, lost the dearest thing in my possession because I valued it too highly.

The gods who fling to us their own gift of love must wring their hands, or split their jovial sides with contemptuous merriment to see how we poor mortals use it. Some flee from it, some to it, some stamp on it, some clutch it, while others throw it away.

My twenty-two years of living had left no more impression on things or people than a breath of air. I felt that had I died then, or run away to the mountains as I craved to do, and hidden my demented self among the clouds and crags instead of thinly veiling it in my own undesired flesh, none would have missed my presence or marked my absence more than a single dewdrop. Nothing vital quickened me; the seeds of passion, the power of devotion remained uncherished and ungathered. Peace, peace, peace, heavy solitary, slighted peace, after no struggle, no gain, no victory, no harvest: the peace of poverty. I was exhausted without possession; I was worn without wear. The days passed dully. I dusted, swept, put flowers into vases, taught Dorothea, played with her, walked with her, bathed her, put her to bed in her little railed cot which had been mine, over which I used to stretch my arms and call to our French nurse 'Please lift me out: it is morning now,' and she with her black hair in a tangle, stirred, sat up and, rubbing the sleep from her eyes, took me in her plump white arms and carried me to her bed where I snuggled into her neck.

While I combed the little girl's pale fair hair and tucked the blanket round her, my cousin sat in the nursing chair bathing the baby who was only four months old. The fat creature chortled, wailed and kicked. She churned the water, grinned and yelled for her supper, and afterwards her mother, a half smile on her mouth, fed her, turning her head over her shoulder to read a novel on the table beside her.

Dorothea played with scissors and pieces of rag, the baby gurgled, the nursery was always in a litter. And sitting in the window-seat looking out on the yard below where the ducks marshalled themselves in a row, and beyond the buildings to a steep hayfield glinting with a silvery light on the growing grass, I felt utterly forlorn and thrown upon myself. I stayed up very late at night, and rousing myself long after the others had gone to bed, I frequently saw that it was two in the morning. The ashes in the grate were cold. Whose good had I studied during those over-the-fire meditations? Nobody's.

I played the gramophone. Many of the records were cracked, the needles rusty, and the instrument was old. I found Chopin's 'Fantasia Impromptu'; it wove a pageant in the chilly room: how brief a time it lasted, and with the music the wonder fled; how blackly the night enclosed the lighted room, seeming to lean on the uncurtained panes with a weight that I felt. I was the last stronghold of wakefulness; sleep pricked my eyelids and paralysed my limbs. Stubbornly I fought it: I wished to be so tired that thought became impossible, thought that went round and round in my head on the same old track, round and round like a donkey drawing water. I would never go to bed before morning.

I used to stare at *The Times* till the print blurred before my eyes, or take out and turn over the books in the shelves. They did not interest me, and I did not read them, but looked at them and put them back. Sometimes I studied the pictures on the walls, or if I sat in the drawing-room where there were none I handled the old china, or swept up the hearth till not a speck of ash or coal lay on the tiles and even the logs were meticulously sorted and piled in sizes. From three gilded mirrors Arabella watched me, heavy-eyed and stealthy, tired . . . dog tired. . . .

My feet were cold. The moments passed. Each seemed an age, and yet they passed. I had been to Witstowe; the church was full of flowers. There I was sad; the town was market merry. There I was sad, even in the sunshine.

I turned out the lights and went upstairs. Passing my cousin's room I heard their voices, and the baby whimpering. My bed was cold, too. In the daylight I should wake, should not be able to see the end of the morning before me, yet it would soon be over. Patience.

Before I slept a queer mood of homesickness assailed my drowsing consciousness, a longing not for my people but for the trees and lanes and fields I knew.

The first fortnight dragged away. The rain poured, the winds rocked the trees and moaned in the chimneys as though it were March instead of May. We went for dreary walks between dripping hedges, clothed from head to heel in macintoshes and gum-boots. Sometimes we took the baby with us; safe and dry, she slept under the pram hood, or stared with round, misty eyes at her black sky; when I wheeled her over a rough or stony road and she felt the springs underneath her little body, she smiled or slept, but more often she cried, for she was spoilt. Then Dorothea, running beside in a tiny blue serge jacket and a tight-knitted cap like a helmet, pushed her head beneath the hood and adjured her sister seriously:

'Laugh, Di, laugh.'

The creases smoothed themselves from the pink cheeks and the contracted forehead, for a moment the baby's face would be fair and sweet and placid, while the serious gaze fixed on the little girl, then it broke into a thousand dimples. . . . Dorothea sprang to the roadside and tore flowers from their roots, dandelions and buttercups which she stuck into the crack between the pram and the pillow. In the middle of the month the sun shone, the clouds dwindled on the

horizon, the fields were yellow with cowslips and buttercups, from every apple-tree blossoms snowed down upon
the ground, the young wheat and the pushing grass rippled
in the wind. Reflections were broken, light glanced, darted
among fresh leaves blowing on the boughs. Sap rose, birds
reared second broods. But . . . there were no strong hills.

*   *   *

The baby would not go to sleep. Her face scarlet, she lay
in her cradle screaming furiously. I lifted her out, put her
over my shoulder and patted her back. She hiccupped and
became quiet. I walked up and down the bedroom in the
evening sunshine, holding her. At first, knowing and understanding nothing of babies, I had been afraid to touch her,
now I was quite used to it. I put her back in the cradle
carefully, and kept my hand beside her head. She had
straight white hair. I rocked gently, feeling sorry for her, but
the rocking was a nuisance because in the few minutes before
dinner I wanted to write.

I wrote for my distraction, using as a background the
countryside in which I had grown up: my characters I
had known since childhood. Gradually my creations, these
puppets with a strange wilful life of their own, took complete possession of my imagination. I could not tell where
truth ended and fiction began; I discovered what a pleasure
I could find in blending the two.

At school they had often told me that I could write. My
headmistress said in her opinion I should be a fool if I gave
it up. Her view was not shared by me, nor by my mother, a
sufficiently severe literary critic who gave me no encourage-
ment in that direction.

Some two years previously I had made an abortive effort
to set down the same story; disliking the result I abandoned

it. But the manuscript had survived. Finding it among my music, I had packed it in the bottom of my trunk. One evening I began to take it to pieces, and put it together afresh; from the first it took on new impetus, I felt a new power flow through my mind, and born of my humiliation, a new fierce eagerness to accomplish something that might not be considered or described as childish and puerile.

The evenings were long; I had no desire for company. After dinner I went upstairs to my room, and standing, leant my weight on the high window-seat. Among the pencils, tubes of paint, palette, brushes, knitting and books, I found my fountain pen and, unscrewing it, travelled at once to green places where I had grown. Dusk closed in. I was almost happy, almost serene. Almost.

In my bitterest moments I had come to the conclusion that it was possible to be happy before loving, perhaps after, but never while that diabolical poison coursed through the veins.

The whole wide yard lay under my eyes in the fading light; I heard sleepy cheeping and the beating of clumsy wings in the hen coops and the fowl runs; three kittens chased one another noiselessly, the mother cat curled on the wall stared blankly at them. She stretched, yawned and thrust her head into the pig bucket. Directly beneath the window the kitchen door opened and the maid slipped out to meet her sweetheart in the lane; her straight, lithe legs bent a little seductively at the knee as she walked, she had removed her cap and shaken out her brown hair. I paused to watch her out of sight. One evening when I was standing at my window the sky turned a dark, livid green, the atmosphere grew dense and menacing, and then the rain swept down like a curtain. A boiling stream flowed through the yard, the small, busy animals fled to the barn for shelter; the ducks lifted up their heads and shook their tails. The

bad spell broke . . . in the wait before the storm the earth
had lost its familiarity and taken on the semblance of an
evil dream where monstrous shapes might stalk, lurking in
the heaviness. The rain roared on the roof and ran down
my window like a river; it was too dark to write. I felt a
strange excitement; the conviction swept over me that what
I had written was good, better than I had ever done before.
I said with harsh haughtiness:

'He shall be seen by my light.'

Sometimes I wrote during the day. Once when everybody had gone out and the baby had been left in my care
I became so absorbed in what I was doing that I did not
notice the rain was pouring on her as she lay asleep in the
garden. I rushed to the pram; she had opened her eyes and
was just beginning to cry. Suppose she should have croup?
Hastily I wheeled her indoors, wiped her dripping little
face, walked in the long passage, holding and hushing her
in my arms while the pillow and blanket dried on the
radiator. On the parents' return she was warm and dry again;
I did not tell them of my carelessness. Indeed, I began to
feel now more than ever before that confession was foolish
and to be found out contemptible. That belief cut me off
from all but superficial contact with other people.

Heavily, heavily the days trundled by. I was glad when
the hours passed quickly and the evenings came. I strained
my eyes ahead, tugged at the leash . . . for what?

*   *   *

The churchyard was separated from the garden by a low
wall and a small field where young colts were turned out
to grass. They used to gallop wildly up and down, and roll
under the lime trees snorting and biting at one another's
legs. I saw an old woman's funeral. The bell tolled harshly,

the people filed slowly along the paths carrying flowers and shaking hands: I could see the mound of thrown-up earth: it was stony and pale yellow in colour. A woman adjusted her spectacles to read the names on the wreaths, the vicar's dog, who had crawled through the wire netting that surrounded the churchyard, sniffed at the feet and gazed around him lifting his ears.

After the service the crowd quickly melted away. I heard a car in the lane, then the sexton began to fill up the grave. Earth to earth.

Had that woman, once young and quick as I, had she ever counted her numbered hours, had she tried to 'pass' her limited time? She lay there.

I found something rather ludicrous in the solemnity, and the vicar intoned the service with relish.

That same night Dorothea walked naked on the rim of the bath, hands above her head lightly pressing the ceiling with her flattened palms, balancing, one foot placed before the other, her toes opening and shutting, her pink tongue out. What grace, what beauty in that child's body, her perishable body!

The 'Unfinished Symphony' was to be broadcast. After I had shut up the chickens and chased the ducks into their pen I went into the study to listen. There were several people sitting and discussing William's novel. Blissfully and heedlessly they chattered through the giant-striding chords, the unearthly melodies, those faint, receding footsteps, dropping into distance like averted doom. He that hath ears to hear, let him hear . . . if others will permit him.

I took leave of the company, and went for a walk. It was about half-past ten and the moon was mounting in the sky; the church threw a hard, black shadow, the fields were white with marguerites. A light mist hung over the river and the water meadows. I felt a doleful lassitude; the heavy

dew soaked my cold feet to the bone. Against a haystack a
man and woman leant with their arms round each other's
necks absorbed and lost in their passion.

I did not want to die – there were many things that
interested me – but I did wish that I had never been born.
I thought of the Wooden Doctor who had grown into my
miserable heart as my very flesh. 'I must go to the mountains . . . oh where shall I go, and how shall I live? Running
through the long grass my shadow fleeing before me, I
could find no answer. Two swans resting in the reeds
frightened by my violence swam to the middle of the river;
snow-white, tranquil, they pushed against the stream. 'Papa,
what inscrutable law of Providence brought you into my
life if you were not to love me? With you, for you, I might
have been good, might have come to my full strength.
Without you there is nothing . . . nothing.

'Why must I trample on this one pure passion?

'Oh to be away, alone. I'd like to look through my *own*
window, I'd like when it grows dark to creep up to my own
bed, I'd like to tend plants in my own garden, to watch the
seasons pass, and return . . . alone, always alone, since you
are not beside me.'

My cousins were a devoted pair. Contented with my sole
friendship, secure in its protection, I had looked out on other
folk indifferently, or had expended the easy compassion
with which one is born; now bereft of my own happiness,
I fiercely resented the feast spread all around me which I
could not share.

Never in my existence had so many happy people surrounded me; my cousin smiled, radiating joy and fulfilment, the children romped and roared with glee, good
spirits and good temper, the village seemed a posy of merry
faces. The envy and jealousy in my soul marched black,
thunderous and undetected: I too smiled, a dissimulating,

disguising smile that hid from them all my raging starvation.

The beginning of June . . . and the black dog still tore at
my throat.

There was no sun: the air was thick, heavy and oppres-
sive. Leaves drooped and curled at the edges, the lilac
turned brown, chestnuts and lupins bloomed, gipsies' lace
and buttercups decked the roadsides. The narrow river,
filled to the brim, darted between the orderly willow ranks;
its opaque blue waters delighted my eyes.

Up in the loft my cousin's terrier had a litter of puppies.
I went to make her a bed of straw and take her a dish of
scraps. There among the dust and dirt, the broken boots,
abandoned toys, and battered chairs, I saw upon the floor,
stirring a little in the draught, a butterfly's wing . . . a Painted
Lady's.

The exhausted bitch licked up the food. She looked gaunt
and haggard. Seven smooth, fat puppies dragged at her
with savage energy. I pushed them aside while I laid her on
the clean straw: they crawled back squealing.

As I stood on the loft steps the manor looked like a doll's
house. There were the toy tea-things on the table, the toy
man pumping, the toy cat sneaking through the window. A
great flock of starlings swept across the clear grey sky;
Dorothea with a skipping rope danced down the path in a
bright red frock.

One puppy was saved for me, and I called her Griselda.
The others had their brains dashed out against the wall by
the cowman, except one poor little beast who had been
thrust away from the mother by the others and died. I buried
it, creeping with worms, under a clump of lupins whose
sweet pink spikes were alive with bees.

Men came to strip the ivy off the walls. They worked all
day; in the evening the house was bare. Its blurred outlines

had hardened: it had been a pretty old house, now stark
and grey: it attained beauty. I had so far taken root there
that I felt an almost possessive pride. I entered the study
where my cousin sat sewing. William was with her. They
did not hear me.

Leaning on his elbows, his face shaded by his cupped
hands, he was at his desk reading to her from a book she
held over his shoulder. As she listened, her charming head
bent, she rubbed the back of his neck half thoughtfully, half
caressingly. The needlework had fallen on the floor, strands
of cotton clung to her rather untidy woollen dress, and her
ruffled hair had fallen over the parting.

'You see, dear?' he said, raising his head as he questioned,
so that it pressed against her bent arm.

'Yes, I see, of course. William, it's time Di had her feed.
Are you coming up?'

'Little Di,' he repeated with a kind of controlled rapture,
as if an inner contemplation of his infant daughter prompted
the murmured words, 'Little, little Di.'

My cousin now saw me.

'Here's Arabella,' she observed. 'Well, are you going to
sit up till the early hours? Don't forget to turn off the stairs'
light and rake out the fire. Good night.'

'Good night,' said William.

'Good night,' I answered.

They mounted the stairs. A door slammed. Dieu, sois
apaisé: aie pitié de moi.

*   *   *

Did I mean to cheat the publisher? Was it my intention
to convey the impression that I had found a manuscript in
a cottage which was the foundation of my story? Such

appeared to be his opinion. My dear sir, if you read this, and recall the circumstances which I have set down, however incoherently and inadequately, you will perhaps understand why I could not at the time make out a very good case for myself. I might perhaps do better now, but I feel no inclination to try. . . . An ardent devotion offered, politely declined and handed back very little the worse for wear . . . judge me, a woman who will set that down against her own name, who will betray her own passion, and refrain from mocking at it hanging crucified, only because she knows many people who can spit farther and scourge more powerfully. Judge me, whether I meant to cheat you!

'This Arabella,' exclaims the befogged reader, 'how she does indulge herself in mental meanderings! I want a story, I want a hero, not a middle-aged doctor . . . I want a pure, pretty and pursued heroine.' Good person, I am writing a history of humiliation and loss. It is for me: it is mine.

The publisher's letter amazed me: out of the door and down the path I reeled in the sunshine, the same path where two months previously I had read my last letter from the Wooden Doctor. A wild dream, a fantasy had come true.

I had never seriously considered anybody else looking upon my manuscript as more than a rather childish failure; I had found in it a refuge from thought, a cure for nostalgia. Sending it to the publisher was no more than a conclusion, or, to put it plainly, the last dose from a bottle of medicine. And now, like a saucy kite, it sailed out into the blue with the publisher hanging on to the string, saying: 'Yes, yes; you fly well; but are you genuine?'

For my life I could not answer. He must have found me singularly unconvincing at our interview. The atmosphere of his office had a certain severity that afternoon which I sensed with momentary discomfort. My head ached: the fox worried me, and I was still dazed at the discovery that somebody thought I could write. At any moment I could have remarked with perfect truth that I did not care what opinion he entertained respecting my motives.

The story had reached a point when verification had become necessary. The background had shifted from the English to the Welsh side of the Border. Actual information was required to continue; imagination I had not drawn upon, and it would have falsified what had been already carefully described.

The proposition I put to the publisher was sufficiently selfish to fit perfectly into his conception of my character:

If he were favourably impressed by the manuscript would he in payment send me into Wales?

At this point he became very definite: he would not.

I felt dissatisfied and sad. I wished I had not begun the book since I saw no prospect of finishing it.

His last words to me were:

'But you can write!'

And mine (to myself):

'À quoi bon?'

So for the time the matter stood.

*   *   *

In writing this the walls that shut me in from the autumn night recede and vanish: the concentrated heat from the banked-up heap of coal and flame in the fireplace diffuses itself into summer warmth.

The hay was mown and the smell of it, and the sweetness of elder flowers in the hedges weighed on the air. The corn stood high, and where the hay remained uncut, moondaisies grew to my waist. Lupins and delphiniums waved in the gardens. I swam often, and it seemed to me when I had bathed that the smell of river mud and fresh water weeds clung to me all the day.

My cousin was milking. I could hear the pails clanking as I sat on the window-seat in the nursery holding the baby. She stared at me, pleased at the attention; her eyes were very round, blue, and good humoured. The field beyond the wagon house was cut; the grass lay in flat green swathes touched here and there with sunlight. Cocks and hens scratched in it.

My puppy Griselda, grown old enough to waddle, gambolled with a feather in the yard below; the fowls paraded round her fat, rolling little carcase, and every now and then they pecked at her. She looked very puzzled when I called her, high in my window as heaven to her.

My cousin came out of the cowhouse carrying two buckets. She wore her blue overall, and as she crossed the yard to the dairy she glanced up at the window. I held the baby up for her to see.

Dorothea was in bed: for two weeks she had not been allowed to get up. She had a perpetual temperature which we could not get down, although in every other way she seemed perfectly well. Looking at me, she demanded:

'What is mum doing now?'

'She's straining the milk.'

'Will you read to me?'

'If I can keep Di quiet.'

I sat down on the nursing chair, and laid the baby across my knees while I read 'The White Cat' to Dorothea. The little girl's eyes shone with excitement; she flung back her hair and clutched her nightgown. Beneath the blanket her feet beat up and down. The baby began to cry: I jogged my knees and Dorothea screamed angrily:

'Naughty Di, naughty, naughty Di. Be quiet!'

Her face flushed: suddenly she turned very white and

tears filled her eyes. She sobbed, raising her hands to her forehead.

'Dorothea . . . darling, what's the matter?'

'Oh, I feel as though I'm going to die.'

I was very frightened. I put the baby on the bed and ran to the window to call my cousin. She rushed up the stairs, regarded Dorothea's pale face which streamed with tears, and, kneeling beside the cot, took the child in her arms, pressing her head to her breast and spreading her comforting hands over the sharp little shoulders. I brought her the thermometer. Dorothea's temperature had dropped to subnormal.

My cousin felt anxious. She sent for the doctor. He was a tall, lanky man, very neatly dressed; his speech was precise, his manner unbending. His hair seemed as though it had been glued to his scalp, and over the top of his spectacles his black eyes looked out with a kind of restricted geniality. He asked Dorothea solemn questions which she answered panting with laughter and when he left she gave him a red rag doll made by herself out of a bit of her frock, and he put the grinning creature in his pocket.

He told my cousin that Dorothea ought to go to the sea. It was decided that the whole family should have a holiday together. A week later they departed, and once more I went home. Griselda went with me in a small rush basket, wearing the tiniest collar I have ever seen. I tried to brush her for her first journey, but at the slightest touch she fell over and lay on her back. Everybody on the bus admired her, although she climbed down their necks and bit their fur collars.

My mother did not like dogs, but when she saw mine she burst into tolerant laughter.

*   *   *

July passed . . . the first days of August. I found myself
thinking more and more about my book. I had always considered that writing must be a matter of choice, but this
naïve idea turned out to be wrong in every way: the characters that I myself had created clamoured to be let out.
They gave me no peace.

At last I told my mother. She proved both interested and
encouraging. Certainly, I ought to go to Wales.

A great-aunt, a surly recluse of a woman who had given
up what remained of a life that had spent itself in scolding
to harsh criticism, had recently died leaving my father a
little money. My mother persuaded him to let me have
enough for my fare and my board. He was loath to do this,
but my mother observed, 'Take it, he will only drink it all.'
To him she said:

'We have no money to train the children. Help her to
take a chance that may mean a living to her. You must do
something for your daughters.'

My father grumbled, then he suddenly agreed. With
geniality he wrote a cheque and wished me success. We found
the address of a farm in the remoter part of Carnarvonshire; towards the end of August I again left home.

I was glad. I had been afraid that I should meet the Irishman, but except for one occasion when he passed me in a
lonely lane, I was spared.

The journey took nearly all day. At five o'clock I arrived
in Carnarvon, and caught the bus to Abercarrog. The road
ran straight along between the mountains and the sea. The
villages were depressing and ugly, the shore pebbly, flat
and monotonous. My heart sank with every mile.

Griselda, curled up on my knee, chewed her new leather
lead. She had grown double the size of what she was when
I took her from her mother: she had a wiry, rough coat, and
unfortunately she was very dirty in the house.

The conductor came up to me.

'This is Abercarrog,' he said.

A brown, turbid river rushing between boulders coated with green slime ran under the tarred road. The bridge was constructed of large grey flints; at one end there were a few stone cottages with decaying wooden fences and porches, at the other a post office and a grocer's shop with a large plate-glass window where tinned fruit, tinned salmon and tinned vegetables were displayed beside a full bread tray and some coloured sweets. A short distance along the road I saw a cluster of red-roofed bungalows; the surrounding fields were flat and sodden, the hedges had been neatly trimmed to about three feet. The telegraph posts stood out starkly. The bus moved off; a tall boy with a satchel, who had been leaning over the parapet, the sole human being in sight, broke into a flat whistle and, heaving his shoulders, lit a cigarette and spat into the river. I walked a little way; on my left a lane turned up a slight hill parallel with the river, and walking quickly towards me I saw a small woman in a heavy macintosh, wheeling a bicycle. She approached me and greeted me by name. She was Gwynneth Lloyd-Owen from Bodgynan, and she had come to meet me.

She hoisted my suitcase on the fork of the bicycle, and wheeled it staunchly up the hill. Seeing that she scarcely reached my shoulder and the ascent was steep, I felt ashamed, but I could not persuade her to give it up.

A fugitive humour came and went on her face like a light. In her eyes it never went out . . . her mouth was sad. I judged her to be about twenty-seven. It seemed that everyone at Bodgynan was expecting an old maid carrying an untidy manuscript under her arm. Minnie looked at my blue serge and my bare head with approval. She promised Griselda milk and porridge to make her fat. The road became rocky and narrow; I saw the sea blue-grey, breaking on the flat shore in a creamy curve far below; misty clouds rolled down the mountain sides . . .

A young girl ran towards us, her cotton dress blown against her sturdy legs. Gwynneth said:

'My sister Megan. Whatever are you doing out in the rain like this? See, you are wet through.'

'Oh . . . that's nothing,' Megan answered, panting and laughing.

Both girls spoke English well. Gwynneth scowled at her sister's appearance. Her black, very curly hair dripped with rain; as we walked along she took it and twisted it in both hands till the water ran out, then, pulling back the collar of her dress which clung to her body almost as if she had been bathing, stuffed her clammy hair inside it. Her brown legs and arms were bare and rather fat. She had magnificent teeth. She pushed a white gate open and held it for us to go through, snatching meanwhile at an ear of corn and biting it impatiently. The corn on either side of the narrow path reached almost to our necks: we were obliged to thrust it away from us, and at the other end of the field our clothes were almost as wet as Megan's. It was like wading in a golden sea.

A young man in a shirt open to his waist and trousers the colour of earth, frayed and stained and patched all over, strolled behind us swinging a stick and calling to a sheep-dog pup in an obviously roughened voice. Gwynneth said this was her brother John.

'But if we stop he'll run back, so we had better take no notice of him.'

John's long strides, however, soon overtook us. He murmured 'Good evening' in English, though with a strong accent, and turned brick red. At the entrance of the yard he ran into the cowhouse to hide himself.

Bodgynan had whitewashed walls deep as a fortress. The small windows were like tunnels. Grass overgrew the cobbled yard, and there was a straggling, untidy, hen-scratched

patch before the door. Some ragged marigolds, and a thin
apple tree bent almost double, on which teacloths hung out
to dry separated it from a desolate marshy field where
water stood in black, dirty little pools and rushes grew
profusely. Sloe bushes and blackthorn formed a thick, wind-
swept hedge . . . a narrow stream fell over a ledge of smooth
rock. Megan disappeared in the low doorway; she came
out a moment later carrying a pail of potatoes, and began
to wash them in the stream.

Gwynneth took me into the kitchen. Mrs. Owen lay half
on the settle, half on the table, fast asleep; a cat jumped
from her broad back to the floor. I regarded the woman
curiously: she was immensely fat and, like most stout
people, snored. Her mouth was a little open, her cheeks
hung down, and there were creases in her neck as though it
had been tied round in several places with a tight string.
Her hair was taken off her forehead over a pad, but the
pad, slipped from its position, hung over her ear. Her
closed eyelids were a purplish colour. She wore a tight,
brown jumper with a scarlet stripe, a blue skirt and heel-
less bedroom shoes.

'Mam,' shouted Gwynneth. She shook her. Mrs Owen
opened her eyes. They were pale, and very close together.
She sat up, stretched till I thought her enormous bosom
would burst the jumper, opening and closing her arms,
yawning like a cavern.

'What is it?' she lazily asked in Welsh, then, catching
sight of me, she gave me a bright and welcoming smile that
quite transformed her rather repulsive face.

'How do you do, and you must be hungry. I only fall
asleep for a minute while the kettle boils. Gwynneth, she
must be mad to bring you here. You should be in the next
room. Come with me.'

'Can I have a drink?'

'Yes, indeed,' she assented, studying me closely. She brought me some milk which I was compelled to drink in the 'next room,' which had wallpaper, a carved bookcase, and cane tables and chairs decorated with fringed mats and red artificial sweet peas. While I drank, Mrs. Owen looked at me; she was knitting a pair of socks, and her needles flew. She could not speak English very well; some quality in her voice made me sleepy, or perhaps the strong mountain air had gone a little to my head.

*   *   *

My room was little larger than a box. The walls were so thick that to reach the window in order to push it open I had to stretch my arm to its full length. I was tired . . . disgusted . . . I felt that to live or write here would be impossible. Mrs. Owen talked till I wished I were dead. When, at last she left me alone, I heard her haranguing down below in her native tongue. Nobody answered her.

I lay down on the bed, pulled the quilt over me, and slept soundly for three hours. When I awoke, the sun had gone down; my head on the pillow was level with the window, and through it I saw Snowdon standing out solidly against the sky. Footsteps outside tramped to and fro; doors banged, the stairs creaked, I smelt steamed potatoes.

I combed my hair and went down the dangerously steep stairs. A door at the bottom opened straight into the sitting-room where the visitors were having supper. I had forgotten this, and pushed it too violently. The unfortunate man whom it had hit in the back went off into a fit of coughing; his nose had been pushed into his plate. Everyone else kept silent and regarded me reproachfully. The man took his face out of the table-napkin and wiped his eyes. He instantly smiled and observed, 'You see I'm better now,' and rattled his knife on the plate before him. A moment of silence ensued; then everybody resumed an argument, which I seemed to have interrupted, as to where they had been for the day's expedition . . . a girl upset her glass of water in her crumbled bread . . . a man, looking uncomfortably hot, and a woman in a lace blouse entered and sat down at a little table by themselves, turning their backs on us. They talked in whispers, holding their heads down secretively; the man threw pieces of red meat to Griselda. The meal seemed interminable; steam and smoke rose to the ceiling. It grew dark. Gwynneth brought two lamps; she began to clear the table. I followed her to the kitchen. All the family was gathered there for the evening: Mr. Owen, whom I had not seen before, sat at a small table in a dark corner, alone. He was eating porridge. Little of him could be described: his clothes blended with the twilight, but his sharp, pale features, his large, mournful eyes, his high, white forehead, his moving hands, were revealed by a candle flickering in the draught from the door. He wore an old bowler hat tilted very far back on his head. Nobody took any notice of him. Megan ran to and fro carrying crockery to the cupboard; John, leaning against the settle, passed his fingers rapidly in and out of a net which he was making to trap hares. Mrs. Owen, her elbows on the table, seemed more than half asleep: however, when she saw me she asked me to take the armchair by the fire, and, seating herself on the fender, talked to me while, bending forward over her knees, she tickled the back of her neck with a spill. Her face gained an expression both mean and dishonest from her small, pale eyes being so close together. I did not like her, nor her manner, which was bullying, yet conciliatory. I wished that I had not come. Every road I took was wrong . . . suppose I could not write, suppose that was no more than another mistake? Did I think I should be comfortable, asked Mrs. Owen, looking at me narrowly.

'Will there be so many people all the time?'

'No, no, dear; they'll be off tomorrow and then nobody at all till a young fellow for the fishing – a nice young man that comes each year. And you shall have another room . . .'

She made promises:

'You will be very happy. We shall help you – my girls; they are nice girls. They have had good educations. Only nice people come here.'

Mr. Owen began a sentence in a low, timid voice.

'Shut up . . . hold your tongue,' she retorted in Welsh, a kind of purple flush mounting her cheeks. Mr. Owen turned away his head. A cricket began to sing behind the fender. I saw the kitchen dimly through a drowsy mist; my journey, my first sight of the mountains, passed through my mind. I did not hear them go, but when I opened my eyes I was alone; the clock ticking and the crickets singing wove a pattern against the silence; the lamp had been turned so low that the faint blue flame threatened to go out. It was nearly midnight. Griselda stretched herself, ran to the door and whined to be let out. I opened it. A gusty wind blew my frock against me and I felt rain on my face. The cobbles were slippery. I held myself rigidly against the cold air. A few pale stars gleaming in the grey sky looked as though they were caught in the branches of the apple tree. I whistled to Griselda, went in again and bolted the door. Then, turning up the lamp, I spread my books on the table and set to work.

* * *

The next day the other guests left. In spite of my fears, I was peaceful and comfortable at Bodgynan. Mrs. Owen

gave me a larger room where, if it pleased me, I could write
from morning to night undisturbed. Much of my work I
destroyed; at times I despaired and, throwing the manuscript into a drawer, roamed the hills or walked on the
river bank till I felt an irresistible desire to return to my
work.

I wrote in my room at a rickety washstand, dark brown
with age, stained with wet tooth-glasses. My brass bed had
spotted muslin draperies, the floor was covered with
slippery red and green linoleum, a yellow paper bulged on
the walls. The window looked across the orchard: fruit
trees; rough and old, bent to the rank, coarse bluish grass;
between the branches I could see the shore, and Anglesey
milky in the distance. Megan, bare armed, wearing gum
boots, would go into the orchard, frightening the plumed
hens, and shake the trees so that the hard little pale-green
apples fell to the earth. She gathered them into her dress,
then sat on the wall crunching them and throwing the cores
to the pigs. If she saw me she would cry:

'Oh, I'm sorry for you . . . poor thing. I'd rather make
butter!' tossing her hair from her forehead, throwing back
her head. The sunlight turned her brown skin to gold. A
long red mark on her arm gleamed like a weal. She had
fallen off her bicycle.

The two girls did all the work of the house and the dairy.
Mrs. Owen slept, ate, gossiped. She had some idea in her
head that nobody could get on without her: 'My children
can't manage without their Mam,' she observed many
times during the course of a day. She laced herself into such
tight corsets that she was always short of breath, and her
enormous, round bosom, thrust upwards by the constriction,
threatened to fall out of her bodice like pumpkins out of a
basket. She treated her husband very severely, always fed
him on milk porridge and sent him to bed at nine o'clock.

He was not allowed to join in any conversation, nor to move from his particular corner behind the harmonium. His sad eyes followed every movement in the kitchen with a slow, pathetic, intelligent gaze: I remember his childlike joy when he was permitted to take part in a game of whist: his hands trembled over the cards, his gentle, fine features were illuminated by a perpetual smile, and he thrust his beloved bowler farther back on his head than ever. The postman's wife told me his story. He was the last of one of the oldest families in Carnarvonshire. His wife was greatly inferior to him.

Gwilliam Lloyd-Owen, his father, owned a large farm on the banks of the Carrog. A wild, well-to-do man, he left much in his bailiff's hands while he went off for weeks at a time to Liverpool and Manchester on prolonged drunken sprees. The finest looking man in the district, and one of the wealthiest; in spite of his dissipation, many respectable women would gladly have married him, but when he passed his fiftieth year they gave him up for a hopeless bachelor and left him to his own company. Disliking this, Gwilliam disappeared for six months; he returned with a wife, a perfect beauty who bowed down before him in all ways, and finally ran away with a drover. She left a son whose existence became a misery to him. It was said that Gwilliam flogged him round and round the yard with a horsewhip, while the bailiff, a sullen man who cherished an obstinate affection for his master, kept watch at the gate. However this may have been, it was obvious to all that the boy, a thin, stooping, overgrown creature, was abused, downtrodden and miserable. As his mother before him, he found, unknown to his father, or indeed anyone else, a strange outlet for his starved affections in a strong, slatternly dairymaid whose parents had abandoned her in the fields at the age of twelve; it was thought that they had boarded a cargo boat. No great effort was made to trace them; the well-developed child worked for nothing, in fact, she became very useful, and Gwilliam knew her value. She wiped up Trefor's blood and tears through childhood and, when later he discovered other needs, she fulfilled them in the barns and the cowhouses, or in summer under the hedges. Gwilliam discovered them; he always carried a heavy stick, and with this he struck the boy so hard on the head that he fell to the earth as if he were dead. Sian, who had been standing sullenly regarding her master, sprang forward as Trefor fell, stung from lethargy into the sudden realization of her own formidable strength. She tore the stick from the amazed old man. He looked up, saw death brandished above his brow, and quailed.

'Don't kill me,' he said.

'If he is dead, I will,' she replied and, keeping her eyes on him so that for his life he dared not move, she dropped on her knees beside Trefor. After a minute he struggled up on one elbow; Sian took his bleeding head on her breast and glared defiance at Gwilliam.

'You can marry him,' he said, and was suffered to depart.

They were married. Gwilliam, before his death two years later (he was drowned in a flood), put them into Bodgynan. They had seven children who played on the doorstep in rags and dirt while Sian scratched her elbows and slept. The eldest girl, Gwynneth, brought comfort and order into the house and acquired a careworn expression before she was well into her teens. Trefor found that he had exchanged a taskmaster for a taskmistress, but he was born without rebellion in his heart and suffered meekly. Only in John the ancient blood betrayed itself: he inherited his father's noble features and dignified gestures; his wide-opened, dark eyes were magnificent and dreaming. He was an artist. A few pencil drawings of rabbits feeding, sheep on a mountainside, and stoats playing by the edge of a wood, were nailed to the kitchen walls. They were his.

*   *   *

Now that the last summer visitors were gone, Gwynneth put the chain on the front door, polished the parlour floor, and laid the artificial flowers away in a box. The fishermen, they told me, lived just like themselves; they were very simple in their tastes though they were wealthy and used to the best of everything. Everybody looked forward to their visit.

'We shall have some good fish,' said Megan, smacking her lips; she glanced in the mirror and ran her hand over her shining hair. Gwynneth turned down her mouth:

'Mr. Austen talks more than he catches,' she retorted, 'to my mind he's all tackle and no catch.'

Megan laughed, and ran away to the dairy.

We heard her singing the 'Ash Grove.' Her spirits soared. The days passed tranquilly, drawing in towards autumn, the long evenings approached. At night, after everybody was in bed, I sat close under the tall glass lamp with the red curtains drawn and the fire dying in the grate. The only sounds in the kitchen were the crickets singing and the cats rustling the newspaper which Gwynneth spread over the fender. But when I opened the door to let Griselda out I heard the murmuring water in the darkness and it spoke of measureless desolation encompassing this kitchen comfort, of wet and solitary fields, of bare, windy mountains, of black pools reflecting the stars, and bending sighing rushes.

With the early hours a grey weariness fell upon me.

*   *   *

One Sunday a famous preacher came to the chapel at Abercarrog. The whole family went to hear him. After the service they returned with the minister and his wife and daughter, who were to spend the night at Bodgynan.

The minister, Gruff Davies, pale and exhausted, sat in the armchair in front of the fire with his feet on the fender. A flame still burnt in his eyes, he spoke little, his brow was bent as if the contemplation of sin afforded him pain rather than the prospect of salvation promised him consolation. His wife carried supper to him . . . he would not eat, and she looked at him from time to time in a steady, apprehensive kind of way. The tea was made: Megan, her Sunday sleeves rolled up to her shoulders, her head swinging, leant over the fire, frying the sausages.

I, too, looked at the minister; his sunken face possessed a charm that made it difficult to remove one's eyes . . . humour lurked beneath the lines; humanity lay on the broad, high forehead, resolution in the short, sharp chin, more than a touch of mockery in the twisted mouth. A strange face for a preacher.

He drank two cups of black tea, drew a long breath and began to smoke a pipe. Then, without turning his gaze from the fire, he addressed me:

'Well, young lady, you have been looking at me a long time – what do you make of me?'

'Oh, I might answer you in a hundred different ways.'

'A new specimen, eh?'

'Not altogether.'

'Come now, tell me. You needn't flatter me . . . my father was a cobbler, my poor old mother couldn't read or write. I've worked in the mines and split stones on the roads. My susceptibilities are not tender. You write books; do you think I look like a Welsh minister should?'

'No, I don't.'

He had turned his face towards me leaning his head against the chair back . . . he had a tormented expression. I saw that one hand, hanging down by his side, was clenched till the knuckles were white. Mrs. Owen leaned across him to place the teapot on the hob. She remarked:

'Mr. Davies is the best preacher in North Wales. It's a grand man.'

The minister laughed and knocked out his pipe.

'Will you take her word for it?'

'I don't need it.'

'Who are you, girl? I see a spark in your eyes, and I never marked such a jaw on a woman's face before . . . it will clear a path wherever that brow may lead you. The nose . . . there's the weakest part of the face . . . but how charming!'

'You find me attractive?'

'I do . . . and dangerous. Ah, you laugh, but laughter can't hide your black brow, though it's the best mask you can find perhaps?'

'I don't want a mask. I am as you see me.'

'I'm aware of that. Are you angry; have I offended you? No, you smile, and how sweetly. Most would think I am taking a devilish liberty . . .'

His wife stared at us in astonishment. She held her knitting, but she only ran the needles through the carefully arranged grey curls on her forehead with solemn perplexity.

'Gruff,' she asked, 'are you tired?'

'Yes,' he said, moving his shoulders.

'Would you like to go to bed?'

'No, I am very comfortable.'

He shut his eyes. 'When 'I do this I seem to see a full chapel before me, and all the gaping faces, row upon row. Sing to me, Blodwyn.'

His daughter, a girl of twelve, twisted her hands on her lap. Her lip trembled.

'What, thou art frightened?' he continued in Welsh.

'No,' she whispered.

Gwynneth went to the harmonium. As the notes swelled through the kitchen, Blodwyn suddenly flung herself into the middle of the room, threw up her thin arms and passionately burst into song. Her voice was shrill and piercing, like a pipe; she was young, she had bushy, golden hair standing out from her neck, and she wore a white dress resembling a tunic . . . as a bardic spirit of the days when her song was new she seemed; the torrents' rushing rung in her childish voice, the breath of old Wales lay on her lips, its heart beat furiously in her breast. I saw a pulse throb at her throat, and her eyes alight with ardour. She made me think of the bubbling Carrog flowing over rocks, down to the Irish sea.

When she had finished every cheek was flushed. She knelt on the floor beside her father. He put his arm round her shoulders.

'We are not yet dead,' he said softly, and added: 'When I was a boy I used to climb Snowdon and look down into Nature's very heart. If there were a storm at night I left my father's roof and ran among the desolate rocks in the pouring rain and darkness to see the lightning play below me . . . the clouds dissolved on Eryori, and the heavenly fire descended. My poor old mother beat me . . . I couldn't feel her blows, but I used to roar aloud. The last tanning she gave me she could hardly lift her arm. I thought of those nights when you sang, Blodwyn, and my blood ran quicker. Well . . . all that is over now.'

The child sang again, slowly and sadly . . . 'All through the night.' Everybody but Megan joined in the last verse. She sat apart, her eyes lowered, her face in shadow. She wanted to go to Liverpool, she wanted many things that she could not have at Abercarrog. She dreamed, perhaps, of

streets and lamps and tall buildings, or high heels, silk stockings and curled hair, sitting there so silently withdrawn in
mute disparagement; and the minister, of what did he dream?
And the minister's wife sitting counting her stitches? And
Mrs. Owen asleep on the settle . . . John making his net?

One by one they went to bed. Rousing himself long after
the others were gone, the minister rose, and began to walk
up and down the kitchen in a restless, disturbed manner.
He was very pale, the look of suffering had returned to his
face. As he passed the table he touched my manuscript and
I laid down my pen, for it was impossible to write.

'Tell me, do you find any satisfaction, any fulfilment in
writing a book?' he asked, pausing beside me.

'I find it terribly hard.'

'Then why do you do it?'

'Because I must.'

'I know, I know,' he exclaimed with strange excitement,
'you are driven. . . . We are all driven, till at last we go over
the edge. There's no escape. . . . I begin to see it now – do
you think it odd that I should speak like this?' he inquired
in a calmer tone.

'No; but sit down. You are so restless, and I have to crane
my neck to talk to you.'

The preacher dropped wearily into a chair. He leaned
across the table, searching my face with a brilliant yet jaded
glance.

'When I was a boy,' he said slowly, 'it was all so simple. I
knew right and wrong, bad and good. Now . . . oh God,
they look to *me* for truth! I cannot see, I cannot see.'

'I can't offer you any consolation.'

'You speak drily. There's comfort in that composed cold
voice: I have heard so much of fiery eloquence. I have
preached life after death for so many years, promised it,
sworn to it, looked forward to it. And now I see Eternity

stretching out before me . . . for ever I see it in my sleep, an endless waste, and all I want is rest.'

My heart throbbed with pity. I stretched out my hand across the table and took his.

'Come out into the air.'

A warm breeze flew across the damp fields. The hill beside the farm rose a sombre, sinister hump against the greyish sky, the moon gave a watery light. We walked slowly along the field path between the rustling oats and the thorn trees. It had been raining; drops fell on us from the branches as we passed underneath, the wet corn brushed against us. It was midnight.

'You are tired?' observed the minister, noticing my lagging step. 'You ought to be asleep.'

'On the contrary, I never go to bed before one.'

'Ah, you have led an artificial life . . . your world isn't my world. I see plainly—'

'What is your world?'

'This.'

He made a wide gesture.

'Mine also. I have lived all my life in the country. I have no desire for artificiality – for towns.'

'How can one write a book without that?' he demanded naïvely.

'Just as easily as one can preach a sermon.'

'Fatally easily . . . but when the book is written, or the sermon preached, is anybody the better for it?'

'Yourself perhaps. Anyhow, that doesn't matter.'

He murmured something under his breath of which I could only catch one word – despair. And desperate he looked in the wan light. Suddenly I was frightened, frightened of the emotion that was rising in me, coming to life again with dreadful pangs. I was waking! I turned, not sauntering now, but walking fast and keeping my eyes on the ground. The minister followed me without question or remark as though he too had felt something threatening. In the kitchen we regarded each other almost guiltily.

'Good night,' said he, hastily, 'I have kept you from your work. Forgive me.'

'Not at all. Good night.'

After the barest pause he added:

'Give me your hand. You know I shall not see you in the morning.'

I held it out. He kissed it twice and left the room.

Months later I heard of his death, which occurred while he was preaching to a large congregation at Cardiff.

I went to my room, undressed and put out the candle. I lay thinking . . . while the breeze stirred the curtains and fluttered the pages of my manuscript, thinking:

'What is going to happen to me?'

*   *   *

The next day the fishermen arrived – for Oliver Austen brought a friend with him. His name was Bayard.

After walking on the hills all the afternoon I returned and found them in the kitchen. Oliver was so tall – six foot four – that his head almost brushed the rafters. I saw a young man of twenty-five or so, splendidly built with a pale, triangular face, small ears and curiously bent, black eyebrows that, sweeping downwards from the temples almost to the bridge of the nose, gave him a rather sombre expression in spite of the laughter that illuminated it. His thick, longish hair was very fair, his eyes hazel, having that quick glancing regard peculiar to eyes of this colour, like water running over brown pebbles. Megan introduced us: we shook hands, smiled slightly, and accepted each other conventionally.

Mr. Bayard must have been more than twice his age. His figure possessed no grace; he had lumpy shoulders, long arms and was remarkably bald. He carried his head forward; one hand was always hidden in his pocket. I liked him immediately. His fisherman's enthusiasm far outstripped Oliver's, as did his skill and patience. He gave me 'Red Ike' to read. It was refreshing after Alan Raines' unrealistic sentimentalities which were all I had found at Bodgynan. It was the right time and the right place to read a poacher's tale. I took off my coat, which the rain had soaked, and hung it up. It was very dirty, stained with paint, and reached to my ankles. Oliver stared at me quizzically. My hair was wet: I shook it out and Mrs. Owen roused herself to rub my head; her pants and snorts made me laugh, and Oliver exclaimed:

'Why, you have a dimple!'

He seized Megan under the arms and danced her round the kitchen till they were both completely out of breath. I thought him stupid and rowdy, but I could not help looking at him. He possessed a most rare accuracy of form. His muscles, as far as I could judge, were in disposition: and development nothing short of marvellous. What a model!

He thought me plain and smug. He told me so later. I supposed that his continual glances at me were directed against my faulty features. Our eyes met repeatedly as Mrs. Owen jogged my head up and down: my face was scarlet. I thought she would break my neck.

'Thank you,' I said, grasping her wrists, for she rubbed absolutely like a machine and seemed to have no idea of leaving off. I shook back my dank hair and went away to put on a dry skirt. From my window I saw Oliver, Mr. Bayard and John set off for the river carrying their rods. Oliver was singing loudly and cheerfully.

From the first we were antagonistic: the few words we

spoke were constrained, our smiles were false, our glances sharp and probing; we sat as far from one another as possible. One evening Griselda got at his tackle: she loved to pull things to pieces, and in five minutes while we were having supper she had dragged a line all over the floor in a hopeless tangle. Oliver seized her by the collar. I thought he was going to beat her, but he only held her up and laughed into her frightened puppy-face with its hanging pink tongue and rolling sparkling eyes.

'What's this?' he said, suddenly, 'she's torn her pad. It's a bad place, it ought to be washed.'

And he looked at me rather sternly as though I had neglected her. It was true that I had been occupied with my writing nearly all day and had hardly seen Griselda, who spent her time playing with Connor, the sheep-dog pup, outside the door. Gwynneth told him this.

'It's a pity,' he observed. He washed her foot himself. After the table was clear I gathered up the line and began to try to untangle it. Oliver sat opposite me also busy; he did not speak to me at all, but turned his head over his shoulder, laughing and talking with Megan, who stood behind him leaning her folded arms on the settle, her white teeth worrying her underlip.

He seemed very fond of her. I thought she was in love with him.

*   *   *

One fine afternoon I walked to the church at Bryn Carrog, meaning to draw the font, which I had been told was remarkably fine. Mrs. Owen gave me a basket in case I should see any blackberries on the way; I found plenty, and picked the basket half full. Setting it down in the church porch, I entered and found the place empty.

Sunshine flooded the bare, whitewashed building. It shone on the carved oak screen as I have seen it shining on brown leaves in autumn. This natural effect appeared so voluptuously beautiful in its severe and chaste setting that I could only stand and gaze and marvel. Rich decorations, stately pomps there were none. No crucifixes, no heavy cloths stiff with gold thread, no flowers withering on the altar, no stained glass tempering daylight to an enervating dusk. Beyond the clear diamond-shaped panes I saw the blue sky and some branches of ivy tapping against the windows.

I walked round the church. The font was indeed very old and curiously carved; it was, however, far beyond my powers of drawing and, stooping to look at the figures I had just come to the conclusion that I must be satisfied with a close examination, when I heard a man's footstep in the porch behind me. I stood up; it was Oliver, who was very calmly eating the blackberries, holding the basket and picking out the ripest.

'What are you doing . . . eating my blackberries?'

'Do you mind? I'll replace them for you.'

'Blackberries don't grow among the tombstones.'

'But probably there are more where these came from. Have you any objection to my walking back with you?'

'Yes. I'd rather go alone.'

He broke into laughter and advanced into the church.

'Somehow,' he said softly, though not whispering, 'somehow this is the last place in the world I should have expected to find you.'

'Were you expecting to find me?'

'Hardly . . . we aren't on terms of such intimacy. But there are some places where you would appear indigenous. On the mountains, for instance – or in Montparnasse. Here, you look like a pirate.'

I smiled at him sourly: 'Stop a minute, monsieur, not so fast. Do you think I shall let that remark pass unchallenged?'

'I'm very certain I could not make any remark that you wouldn't question. We're bad friends, aren't we? I wonder why. Let us go home and discuss it on the way.'

'What is the use of that?' I asked as we left the church-ard, 'Better pick blackberries.'

'Not at all, we might thresh the matter out.'

'I'm tired of talking.'

'You can't make friends without it,' observed Oliver.

'Why make friends?'

'My dear Miss Warden, you must, you are bound to . . . wherever you go. With your charm of manner!'

We laughed antagonistically. Our glances clashed and we both flushed.

'If you were a little smaller it would be absurd,' he said, looking down at me and reaching out in a haphazard kind of way for a cluster of blackberries. He picked them and threw them carelessly into the basket.

'You know I don't admire you at all,' he continued, 'you're a nondescript height, neither commanding nor appealing, and you have a wild, lost air. No, you don't attract me.'

'Pirates don't attract, they capture.'

'Heaven help me, is that your idea?'

'Yes.'

We walked on hurriedly without noticing in the least where we were going. The track was strange to me, winding between low thorn-bushes and almost overgrown with bracken; a hill in front of us hid any prospect. Oliver went first; he held the long sprays of bramble out of my way, and though there were plenty of blackberries he did not think to pick any.

'I hope you know where we are.'

'I do; we shall come to the river in a minute. This is one of my short cuts,' he replied over his shoulder, 'you'll have to let me carry you across.'

'That's romantic. Did you plan it?'

'It's all part of the treaty. I have thought of nothing else all the way.'

'There'll be no treaty,' I cried, grasping at saplings, grass rocks in reckless descent to the river bed, thirty feet below.

'Hallo, what are you doing? . . . don't be a fool . . . you'll hurt yourself,' he shouted.

Stones rolled away under my feet. They fell splashing into the shallow, swift water.

'Arabella, come back . . . you can't cross here, you'll be carried down to the pool. God, the little idiot's done it!'

He plunged in after me. The current was appallingly swift the slippery, weedy boulders afforded no foothold. . . . I felt no fear of drowning, but I thought, 'Tomorrow I shall be black and blue all over. What has happened to the basket? and oh, how bitterly cold!'

In midstream a large jagged rock stood boldly forth green with slime, parting the water into two boiling white cascades. I reached that rock, how, I cannot tell, and pulled myself up. I was wet to my waist, my head was spinning – the trees on the bank, the water's glide and leap, the green, flat field beyond were blurred in my sight. I saw Oliver's two hands grasping the jutting point, and his raised face. He was pale: his eyes were wide open with astonishment and alarm.

'Why did you do that? Now we *are* in a fix. You'll have to let me help you,' he said.

'I refuse absolutely—'

'You must. Please, dear.'

I stood up, spread my arms and leapt as far as I could. Naturally I fell; the current rolled me over and over. Oliver seized me by the shoulders and lifted me to the bank. I was not in the least faint, though terribly cold; for a moment I could not see and he put both arms around me. After a moment I looked up at him; his expression was dark, strained, his arms unclasped; he spoke in a flat, weary voice:

'Come, let us go home,' he said.

*   *   *

Mr. Bayard left the following day. We were all sorry, but as we stood near the car, Oliver and I felt excited. We waved our hands; the car bumped along the cart track, and when it had disappeared we turned to each other mutely questioning the future. In the field the oats stood ready to be carried; for the first time I saw John out of temper. He was in a passion. Furiously he denounced the young manhood of Wales . . . there they were propping themselves up against the walls in Bryn Carrog, drawing the dole, ogling the girls, and speaking English. 'Speaking English, among themselves! All of them, and none to help us with the harvest.'

The farmers were obliged to help each other. A neighbour came to Bodgynan to give them a hand. His name was William Lloyd, and he was a fat, red-faced, grizzled man. The pupils of his light blue eyes floated in the whites; they were always very wide open and nothing seemed to escape them. His wife had married him to acquire a farm which she loved, because, as a child it had been her home. She might have made a worse bargain . . . gossip said not easily.

Fortunately it was fine. A keen wind blew from the sea tempering the heat, small white clouds sailed in the sky, and the fields and hedges were remarkably fresh for the beginning of September.

I lay on the flat pig-sty roof in the sunshine, writing and watching the harvesters as they trudged up and down the

field. Mr. Owen possessed only one horse, a fat black beast
that drooped its head and walked reluctantly; it always
seemed half asleep. Oliver led it; he was helping John and
Mr. Owen to load; Megan and Gwynneth the stack. Every
time they passed me Oliver cracked the whip, the horse
pricked up its ears and he called:

'There you are still, you lazy girl. Why don't you climb
down and lend us a hand?'

He was very pleased with himself. The wind blew a few
pages of my manuscript into a nettle-bed. He handed them
up to me, grimacing.

'Why don't you come down?' he repeated, 'everybody
else is working overtime while you lie in the sun and watch
us break our backs.'

'Just bring me a few stones, will you, Mr. Austen, and
don't talk so much. You are interrupting the even flow of
my ideas. My work happens to be of a different kind.'

Oliver brought me some pebbles. I placed them on my
papers. He wiped his wet face.

'Work?' he said, 'fine work – writing letters. Can't you do
that later? I ought to be fishing, but it's beyond me to go off
and leave the harvest ungathered. Look at that.'

He pointed to the west where a few white clouds floated
lazily against a hazy sky . . . the sea had a steely rim. 'There'll
be a storm.'

'Oh well, so much the worse. Do go along and leave me.
I'm busy.'

'Busy – you – what are you doing?'

'I'm writing a book.'

Oliver raised his eyebrows; he really seemed interested.

'You are writing a book . . . you? I am constrained to
believe you clever, Miss Warden.'

'Since you won't allow me any beauty, you might credit
me with that, Mr. Austen.'

'I never said you had no beauty. Your mouth is exquisite.
shall kiss it.'

'Now?'

'And you have the most charming manner in the world.
There, is your vanity satisfied?' and he walked away with
he air of one who has come to a great decision.

I was really beginning to be uneasy in his company; uneasy,
yet happy and excited. I could write no more. My thoughts
were not clear, I felt the necessity for movement. As the
wagon returned from the stack I called to them to give me
a ride. Oliver lifted me up; I forgot everything and he
nearly walked into the wheel. He stuck a poppy behind my
ear. I pulled it out. He returned with a cornflower. A seeth-
ing, restless attraction increased between us.

After tea he went fishing. Megan gave me a milking
lesson. I was very afraid that I should be kicked as the
cows seemed restless (a sure sign of storm), but I was
ashamed to own my fear and hid it as well as I could. It
made me angry, too, that Megan could sit unconcernedly
stroking the milk from unwilling udders, while she sang to
herself, or talked casually to John. I felt no fear of the beast
I was milking, but I was terrified that the cow behind me
would put her foot through the base of my skull and crack
it open like a rotten egg. The idea that I am a physical
coward is repulsive to me, yet I fear it is true. There is no
bravery in my composition.

At a little distance from the farm, towards Bryn Carrog, a
broad turf path ran between crumbling stone walls. It was
remote and quiet, an excellent place to walk and think.
Hither I went as the evening approached, more disturbed
in mind than I would have thought possible. The fact was
that I was beginning to search somewhat desperately for
security from my own undeniably awakened emotions. . . .
I seemed to hear in the quietness the Irishman's words: 'In

six months ye will have forgotten.' I had not forgotten,
but was I forgetting? No man on earth would ever take
his place, but was his place as great as I had imagined
it? I remembered the spring, the flowers, the rapture, the
turbulent virgin passion, then the weary summer . . . my
thoughts were not clear, they were like bubbles rising, breaking and leaving no mark, or like pictures in the mind, one
giving place to another in quick confusion. Now I saw
Dorothy de Kuyper at her piano singing of the shortness,
the decay of spring, fixing her green malicious eyes on her
husband; now the Wooden Doctor in his surgery bending
over his desk; now Oliver looking down at me. In fact there
was no end to it – the whole past year rose up before me.

I told myself that I did not like Oliver, that he displeased
me, that he very evidently disliked me. This was worse
than useless; I knew better. The irritability that our sharp
laughter was designed to conceal, the sensitiveness that
discovered offence twenty times in the course of a day, the
urge towards unkindness warned me that I was deceiving
myself. I was forced to admit I had pictured myself in his
arms, and that the bare thought had made me shiver with
pleasure and poignant tenderness. I distrusted my powers
of resistance – indeed, I no longer wanted to resist. As these
disturbing reflections turned ceaselessly over in my head
I experienced such a longing, such a bitter regret, for the
Irishman and his remote yet unutterably confuting friendship, that inevitably I was driven to callousness:

'You fool,' said I to myself, 'why so serious? You don't
matter, and he can take care of himself I should imagine!
He has burnt his fingers already if I'm not much mistaken!
Follow your instinct . . . there's no question of heart . . . that's
over. He said he did not find you attractive, but that's a lie.
Prove it, or try. And let the best man win. No quarter.'

I felt a biting contempt for myself and my undertaking.

The earth refused me sanction, and the heavens would not lend me countenance; the very sweetness in the air undermined my resolution. I was alone in an evening of still, tranquil beauty. The mountains had turned a mysterious milky blue: they stood out solidly, cubist shapes in opaque glass, pedestals to invisible gods. I felt their presence.

*   *   *

Night came. Oliver was still fishing. Nobody spoke, a heaviness brooded on us all, our heads drooped, our eyes closed; only the ashes falling from the grate and the crickets chirping broke the silence. Suddenly lightning flashed across the uncurtained window, dark drops began to run down the shining glass, the rain broke with a roar on the cobbles outside.

Mrs. Owen stretched and yawned. 'This will bring Mr. Austen in.'

She took a candle from the shelf and went to bed. Megan followed her. Gwynneth sat a little while longer, blinking and holding her jaw, which was swollen. She had toothache. Finally, she too went, after setting out a pie on the table and putting the kettle to boil.

The cats leapt to the settle back and purred, tucking their paws under their little round chins. I pulled the curtains . . . I was always afraid that I should look up suddenly one night, should find a face peering in at me, pressed close against the glass, with hair stirring behind it. I could not write. I was alone. Oliver was coming, What would happen?

I heard his footsteps – the latch rattled and he walked in. Griselda went to him; he stooped to pat her. His hair was wet and seemed darker, heavier. He stripped off his waders.

'Are you afraid of thunder?' he asked.

'Of thunder – no. I am very frightened of lightning. It seems to have gone off.'

'Unluckily it has. I hoped I might find you shaking and longing to be reassured.'

'By you? What an incurably romantic man you are!'

'What an amazingly hardy woman you are! You leap across torrents and write novels in a thunderstorm . . . what's this?'

'Pie for you to eat. I'll brew you some tea.'

'I don't want any.'

He fetched a jug of buttermilk from the dairy.

'Have some?'

'No, thank you.'

He drank it, and sat down on the fender. As usual, we disputed; I forget what about: something utterly trivial and absurd. Oliver said that I was obstinate, self-opinionated and stupid. My self-esteem was colossal, I had a diseased ego.

All the time he was talking he looked at the floor and traced patterns with his finger on the hearthrug. I retorted angrily and at random. At half-past one I flagged. Oliver gibed. As much of me as remained awake appreciated, nay, applauded his cruelty, but there was hardly more life in my limbs than in the furry ashes. My skin felt tight over my cheekbones, my eyes felt enormous. I could have slept for ever. I thought: 'I must write.' I said it. The words were my last effort. Oliver took me in his arms; he did not attempt to kiss me, but looked down into my face with a marvellously softened expression. I lay still; poised on the brink of deep sleep I rested contentedly.

'You cannot work tonight,' he said, 'you must sleep. Good night, Arabella.'

*   *   *

The next day I did not see Oliver till the evening, for I spent the day in Bryn Carrog with an artist and his wife who lived just outside the village in a small grey stone house. As I came out of the door the sun was going down, the sky flamed red in the west, a mist was beginning to rise. I walked across the fields by the same grassy track that I have mentioned before and entered the farm as the dusk was falling.

My mood was black and sullen, resentful of I knew not what. I refused to play cards; I beat Griselda, poor puppy, and she lay under the table with pitiful reproach in her golden eyes. Mrs. Owen thought I ought to go to bed, for my head was burning, and I could not read. Everybody else played cards, even Mr. Owen, smiling and passing his hand over his long moustache. They laughed and banged the table; the flame in the lamp leapt up the glass leaving a long smoky tongue, the quivering light glanced on the shiny American cloth which covered the table . . . a design of pink roses and baskets. Megan smiled and smiled. One plump shoulder protruded from her dress, her soft hair framed it. She had kicked off a shoe. . . . Suddenly she threw her cards at Oliver; they glided off him, falling with a patter to the floor. He seized her hands, the dogs lifted their heads, listening and alert.

'Megan, be good,' he adjured her, 'or I'll put you in the bacon rack.'

Gwynneth crept up behind him on the points of her toes, holding a string of onions. She flung them over his head – there was a scrimmage, a chair crashed to the floor.

'Bravo, bravo!' cried Mr. Owen, pushing his hat back.

Oliver swung them up, the two of them. They sat swinging their legs and laughing. 'Now lift Miss Warden.'

He stood over me.

'You dare!' I whispered.

He stooped . . . I hit him hard on the side of the jaw with
my closed hand . . . his face changed. We were in deadly
earnest. He squeezed me to his chest, a fiery current ran
through our veins. Enraged, I could have killed him. When
we were still very young my father had taught us to use our
fists. Girls' warfare was odious, filthy. We called it cowardly;
not in our wildest moods were we ever guilty of it.

I did what I thought to be outrageous even then: with a
ferocious snap I bit Oliver's hand.

He hoisted me into the rack, uttering a furious oath
beneath his breath. I was not ashamed then, but I felt terribly
sick. Blood dripped on the floor. My throat contracted with
passion.

Nobody said anything. They were too shocked. The girls'
smiling mouths took on an almost ludicrous downward
bend. As for Mrs. Owen, her pale eyes nearly started from
her head. After a stifling pause Oliver asked:

'May I lift you down?'

'Keep your bloody fingers to yourself.'

'I will.'

He set Gwynneth and Megan on their feet. I jumped; the
jar ran up my spine, my head throbbed.

I think everybody expected me to leave the kitchen.
Instead, I sat down in my old place by the fire. Oliver went
out into the passage, and the others followed him. After a
moment, John came back, looking at the floor. He called
Connor, opened the door and said, without raising his eyes,
'Good night.' A breath of air reached me, raw and cold and
damp. He shut the door. Upstairs, above my head, they
moved about, pouring water, tearing linen. I brought out
my manuscript but I could not write. The words were stale,
stupid. They had not wiped away the blood . . . impossible
to work with those round, bright spots before me. I took a
cloth, dipped it in the kettle and rubbed at the stones. Then

I sat down at the table; grasped my pen and began to write a sentence . . . pushed everything away. I sat so still that a cricket jumped on me. A cat pounced and ate it, crunchingly. I felt I must see Oliver – must. I longed to clasp and caress the hand which I had hurt, to put it to my breast and cherish it. I heard him on the stairs. He came in wearing a sweater, carrying tackle, and I saw that his hand was bandaged. He regarded me stealthily without turning his head, a furious, burning glance not solely of rage. I would have spoken: the discovery that I could not control my feeling for him made it impossible. He went out. After a moment or two I followed him. He walked slowly and dejectedly about a hundred yards ahead. It was cold and misty and my feet splashed through pools.

The fields looked intensely dreary. I managed to call his name. He turned, waiting for me to come up.

'Well, what do you want?' he demanded roughly and harshly.

'Forgive me, I am sorry.'

Bending, he grasped me by my shoulders; I turned my head, and set my lips to his bandaged hand. He snatched me to him, dragged my head back, kissed me insatiably. My limbs seemed to melt and dissolve in his arms. Alone in the desolate fields we crowded into each other's embrace: with such heedless, hungry strength he strained me to him that I could not breathe . . . I could not see. Yet had I been torn from him then I felt I should have died for want of him; we had starved for each other; now we experienced within us a strong, hot, mutual glow that made us groan. We returned to the farm. The lamplight showed our faces washed with exhaustion, pallid, damp, shadowed. Our eyes burned drily, sunk deep in the sockets like expiring candles.

*   *   *

We were deeply content to be at peace. Cocks began to crow; it was the dawn. Oliver swept my hair from my face and laid his cheek on my forehead. We spoke softly.

'Oliver.'

'Yes.'

'It's getting light.'

'I don't want to leave you.'

'You must.'

'Arabella . . .'

'Yes?'

'You must marry me.'

'I can't.'

'Surely . . . there is no other man?'

'Only a ghost of one.'

'And you won't marry me?'

'I can't . . . I have surrendered up my spirit.'

'Are you laughing or crying down there on my heart?'

'I am not crying. Would you share me?'

'With a ghost?'

'Yes.'

'I would. I would try to make you happy.'

'My happiness doesn't lie in your hands.'

'Are you serious?'

'Oh, Oliver, between us seriousness isn't possible!'

'You can say that now?'

'Yes.'

'My God, Arabella, you're reckless!'

Beyond all doubt the day was breaking. Soon John would be down. Oliver got up and unbarred the door. A wan light penetrated the kitchen. Above, somebody rolled over in bed, coughed, and put their feet to the floor. Oliver came back to me; he took my two hands, drawing me to my feet.

'They are getting up,' I said.

'I know, but listen, my darling, before you go to sleep. Just now I asked you to marry me because I love you, not because . . . this has happened. You do believe me, don't you?'

'I do believe you, Oliver.'

'I offer you tenderness and devotion. You stand in need of both.'

A picture, an instantaneous vision of what our life together might be rose up before me. In time, perhaps, I might love him with my whole heart, never with my soul as I had the Wooden Doctor . . . that was over. Oh, the many ways of loving, once experienced, never repeated! I could not soon answer. I wanted to accept.

'Can't you understand the temptation to take consolation?'

'I can,' he replied. 'Can you understand the joy of giving it?'

'Give me time to think . . . I can't think. It seems so unfair.'

'Don't think now, don't try. Go and rest.'

Bending his head he went out. Griselda stretched, yawning and wagging her mistaken tail. I whispered to her; she jumped up at me and licked my face.

I took off my shoes and crept upstairs. Behind her door Mrs. Owen let out a long breath: 'e-e-e-e-o-o-o-oh' and her bony stays rattled. A jug clinked against a basin. 'Get up,' said Gwynneth's voice, heavy with sleep.

Day had begun.

Undressed, leaning my chin on my hands, I gazed at myself in the glass, seeking a change in the mirrored face. I fancied it was there. Dry, white lips and circled eyes, tangled, matted hair . . .

'Empty,' I said to Arabella.

The day passed tranquilly. We were happy, but towards evening we knew that we were far from satiety.

Oliver was fishing. I sat on a stone watching him.

This deep pool occurred where the Carrog ran through a narrow chasm overhung with twisted trees. It was supposed to be haunted by Roman soldiers who marched along the crag outlined against the sky. Many people at Abercarrog swore that they had seen them often. The place was shunned except by fishermen and shepherds. It was filled with the sound of rushing water, for just beyond the pool there was a big fall where the river bed suddenly dropped twenty feet. It was very dark, too; the twisting, uneven path was dangerous to strangers.

That night stars burnt brightly in the path of sky between the tree-tops, the air was cold and moist. A heavy autumn dew clung to the leaves and beads of the wiry grass and bracken. The air was sharply cold. After a very little while I could no longer feel my feet, though I was wrapped in a rug; I rested my chin on my knees and watched the mist curling up from the pool like smoke, wreathing across the deep black water. A month before a woman had drowned herself in it: she had climbed an alder on the bank and flung herself from an overhanging bough. They had discovered the marks of her feet on the bark, and the twigs bent and broken as though she had clutched at them in falling.

The roar of the waterfall filled my ears. Oliver and I were silent. I felt a sharp pleasure in watching his long, slow gestures. He balanced himself on a little promontory, casting the line far out on the untroubled water – it lay like a thread on the surface. Unconscious, absorbed, he bent, reached and straightened. He was restrained and persuasive.

'It's no use,' he said at last. 'They won't bite.'

I was glad; last night I had bitten his hand almost to the bone, he still wore the bandage; he would probably wear the scar much longer than he would remember me by any other token, and tonight I did not want to see a fish die. He laid the rod on the grass. After a moment he spoke.

'I am going away tomorrow.' He cleared his voice and continued, turning his head away:

'Last night you asked my pardon . . . now it must be the other way about. Can you forgive me, Arabella?'

I listened coldly, bitterly. He meant to leave me.

'Can you?' he repeated. I still said nothing; after all, this was only to be expected.

'You might answer me!' he cried impatiently.

'At least I will do that. Forgive you . . . why should there be any talk of forgiveness? You only acted as I wanted you to act! I want to have lovers . . . you aren't the first.'

'You lie, dear,' he replied quietly. 'I am.'

'I'm going to the devil.'

'I'm going with you. I have been a fool! I began like a brute and went on like a beast. Is it too late for me to begin again?'

'You are going away—'

'I must . . . don't you understand? I love you . . . I want you terribly . . . all the time. You must see that it is impossible to go on like this. Marry me. I'll take care of you.'

He kept his voice low, even cool, but I saw that he was trembling.

'Come to me, Oliver.'

Kneeling on the stone, he gathered my hands into his. He leaned his head upon my knees and shivered. I drew the rug over us both.

'Marry me,' he repeated brokenly.

I felt a rending tenderness, an aching desire to soothe the anguish that the starlight revealed in his eyes. And for my own sake I was tempted . . .

'Yes, I'll marry you.'

And immediately I had spoken I knew that I was happy, so happy that for a long while I was dumb with joy. I saw our future together, and the past fell away behind me.

'Are you happy, Oliver?'

'Yes, oh God, yes. I wish we could stay like this for ever.'

'Are you going away?'

'Yes.'

'Tomorrow?'

'Yes. I am afraid for you.'

He began to tell me about his village in the north. I listened contentedly.

*   *   *

It occurred to me forcefully that there were things I ought to tell him – about my father, and perhaps about the Wooden Doctor. I thought of this as I lay in bed. Then very soon it was morning and I woke up to find him leaning over me.

'Don't be frightened,' he whispered, 'this is the last time I shall see you alone.'

From darkness came the daybreak, from silence his lowered voice. There is with me no confusion in waking. I turned to him. He said gently and sadly: 'I don't know why. I feel as though we were parted already. Asleep, you looked so far away. I have been watching you a long time. Where were you?'

I could not remember. But I did recall my thoughts of the night before as I fell asleep. I sat up.

'Go and wait for me outside. I have something to tell you.'

He looked at me, startled.

'Yes, hurry. I mean it. In ten minutes I'll join you.'

'It's hardly light.'

'So much the better for me.'

He tiptoed out of the room. I dressed in a great hurry, wrapping the paint-stained coat round me like a shawl.

I was surprised to discover that all my happiness of the night before had vanished; it seemed like a dream, like the radiance of a dream which, on waking, causes one such painful disappointment. I went downstairs; the door was open. Oliver was standing by the stream cutting at the water with a stick. It was the action of a boy. After all, he was very young; my heart misgave me. He regarded me gravely:

'Do you know, you have frightened me? Are you going to tell me anything very terrible? Are you going to say you won't marry me?'

'No, no. Of course not. Let's go for a walk. It's so cold.'

'You're shivering. Take my arm.'

It was chilly before sunrise. My hair blew out in the cold breeze. The earth looked pale and unawakened, everything was grey. As we walked across the wet stubble I told Oliver about my father and our savage home. He listened silently until I had finished, then he stopped abruptly:

'Is that all?' he asked and, taking my hand, he added, 'That makes no difference at all.'

I could not tell him about the Irishman. I found no words, and really a man who marries is not concerned so much with the state of his wife's mind before he met her as with that of her body. So I said nothing. Oliver looked at me again; he was smiling now, and he kissed my throat. We stood and watched the sun rise; our shadows mingled, distorted by the rough ground. A copse near us turned green and gold, the pearly sky lightened. It was a subdued sunrise, promising a fine, clear day. But I still felt depressed, perhaps because Oliver was leaving me. 'That's artificial,' I thought, 'I wish we could be natural and free as we were the other night . . . it was divine fire then. They ought to leave us alone until it has burnt out (I could not have defined "they") and then would be the time to separate. Why is he going? I must find out.'

Accordingly I asked him. He said ruefully: 'Because I said I would.'

This amused me so much that I burst out laughing. Then I did my best to dissuade him, but, greatly to my surprise, I found that this was beyond my power. We walked slowly back to the farm. Our real parting took place before we entered, although Megan and I went in the car with him to Carnarvon.

The platform was empty. We walked up and down in the dust till the train came in. I remembered my arrival six weeks before, a stranger seeking wilful seclusion, and now beside me stood the man who would divide me all my life from my own company.

*   *   *

A week later I finished my book. I wrote the conclusion at furious speed, sitting on my bed, my legs curled under me for warmth. The pen scratched over the paper at such a rate that the ends of all the words were quite illegible. My face was hot, my hands freezing; more and more frequently the page flashed, suddenly as though it had been fluttered violently under my eyes, a sign with me that I must stop. The light was almost gone, and the words left the lines. I lit a candle with difficulty, for my arms were cramped. The fox clawed at me . . . I could not move my legs.

With an effort I untwisted my body; a million pins and needles pricked me fierily, my hair had fallen down my back. I had been sitting on the bed for four hours. Now it was quite dark; I had finished. I was filled with triumph and relief. My dead feet stumbling on the littered floor became tangled in heaps of clothes. They twisted round my ankles. I had begun to pack and had forgotten.

The fox ripped my stomach . . . I muttered and murmured to myself. 'Oh, you ugly beast, oh, what a brute you are to torture me . . . this pain is unendurable. I must stop it. Why did I ever consider myself cured?'

But really, in spite of the fact that I could no longer stand upright, I cared very little for the animal; it did not darken my mood. The climb to intellectual or manual dexterity is painful and long, but it culminates in a peak of glory that is touched with the purest light on earth.

I found my pills and crammed them into my mouth one after another . . . then I lay down. Immediately I went to sleep. When the family came to bed I woke up for a moment. Megan had opened the door to find out what had become of me. A narrow line of candle-light shone through the crack. 'She's asleep,' whispered Megan, and the door closed softly. I heard a scratching rattle on the linoleum. It was Griselda. I hung my hand over the bedside; my fingers touched her rough coat.

'Griselda, Countess Griselda, Mouse-Face, here, jump up.' She leapt, and washed my face with kisses. 'Aren't we comfortable together?' She lay along my back, her nose in my hair, and I felt her warm breath on my neck. It was delicious. The next day I left Bodgynan. Mrs. Owen brought out a huge book with brass clasps and I wrote my name in it. It came directly under Oliver's. Megan ran with me across the fields to the station at Bryn Carrog. We were late . . . the train was moving. She pushed me in, we slammed the door. Our hands just touched as she ran alongside with her face upturned. She shouted: 'Come back again!'

'Yes, I will,' I replied, and then we were beyond the platform. The smoke poured past the windows like a woolly cloud. At first I thought of Oliver. We should be married in the spring I fancied. My book was finished. The year had begun badly, it would end well.

Yes, I had forgotten. Surely I had forgotten. The memory of Oliver made me long to be with him.

Shall I write any more?

Yes, though it is difficult.

Difficult because I cannot understand myself: difficult because the longest, slowest thoughts run to no more than a very, very few bare words. But I will try.

Well, then, I thought of Oliver; remembered myself in his arms. We should be happy . . . and the Wooden Doctor had been right; autumn could not mate with spring. I had loved him because I had met no other man who stirred my blood. He knew it, my wise Irishman. I acknowledged the truth of his consolations now. How well he understood the human mind, how far he could see! Everything ended so quickly, so quickly. Pain and the cause of it alike forgotten, years of growth obliterated in a few months.

I put my feet up; the carriage was empty. I felt so secure, so contented that I could safely go on thinking. After a while I went and stood in the corridor. The journey passed very quickly. I had nothing to read but I did not want entertaining. In Salus I did no more than smile at people I knew, for I was in a hurry to be home, until I met the Wooden Doctor face to face. He was walking. He put out his hand:

'Arabella, are ye back again?'

'Oh, Papa—' I stammered.

It looks absurd written down, the conviction that I could not marry any other man. Yet it came upon me just as suddenly.

It only remained to tell Oliver.

*   *   *

All this took place some time ago.

My book was published.

Oliver sends me red tulips on my birthday.

And the Irishman married a young girl a few months after my return.

* * *

And that's the end.